Good-bye Kiss

Kisses

Good-bye Kiss

by Diane Namm

Troll Associates

LIBRARY OF CONGRESS CATALOGING-IN-PUBLICATION DATA

Namm, Diane.
   Good-bye kiss / by Diane Namm/.
      p.   cm.—(Kisses: #2)
   Summary: While working on a fund-raising concert to save their teen
show on a local cable television station, Amanda, Hero, Keera, and
Jamar must also work on their personal relationships.
ISBN 0-8167-3441-0 (pbk.)
   [1. Interpersonal relationships—Fiction.   2. Television—Production
and direction—Fiction.]   I. Title.   II. Series: Namm, Diane. Kisses: #2
PZ7.N14265Go   1994
   [Fic]—dc20   94-16883

Printed in the United States of America.

10   9   8   7   6   5   4   3   2   1

For Kathryn and Michael

Chapter One

*I*t was a swelteringly hot Saturday in August—the hottest day of the summer. But the inside of Amanda Townsend's Cliffside Heights mansion was cool and comfortable, thanks to the air conditioning that was going full blast as Amanda looked through her closet for something to wear.

Today was, perhaps, the most important day of Amanda's life. She and her boyfriend Hero Montoya were going to celebrate their one-month anniversary at Bluff Cove, Amanda's favorite spot in all of Cliffside. Hero's motorcycle was finally fixed, and they were going on a picnic at the most remote spot of the beach. Just the two of them.

After hearing the record-breaking temperature on the news, Amanda chose a gossamer-thin, white, sleeveless summer dress that showed off her smoothly tanned arms and long, sunbrowned legs. The tiny purple rosebud pin in the center of the bodice matched the swirls of violet in Amanda's beautiful eyes.

Underneath the dress, Amanda slipped on a shiny white maillot bathing suit that she'd been saving just for this day. Amanda was hoping to coax Hero into the ocean, even though he claimed to hate the cold waters of the Pacific.

Sitting before her pink-marble vanity mirror, Amanda thoughtfully brushed her long ash-blonde hair, dreamily remembering Hero's gentle touch as he stroked her silky hair and the thrill that went down her spine whenever they kissed. Amanda never tired of thinking of Hero's handsome face and how one lock of soft, wavy brown hair always fell across his forehead.

Since Tyler Scott had challenged Hero Montoya in a terrifying and nearly fatal motorcycle race down Cliff Point Road at the Fourth of July Beach Bash, Amanda and Hero had been inseparable. Almost losing him that night, as he and his motorcycle tumbled down the sheer drop of a hundred-foot slope, had made

Amanda realize how much she loved Hero and how fragile their time together could be.

"Amanda!" Mrs. Townsend's voice broke into Amanda's thoughts.

"Coming, Mom," Amanda called, stepping out of the bathroom to see what her mother wanted.

Mrs. Townsend was dressed in tennis whites, with her hair in a French braid and her tennis bracelet and diamond-earring studs glinting in the sunlight. She was off to the Club to play her weekly game of doubles tennis.

Mrs. Townsend gave Amanda an approving glance.

"You look very nice today, Amanda. Such an improvement over those cut-off shorts and skimpy tank tops you've been wearing lately."

Amanda rolled her eyes and sighed, but her mother simply ignored Amanda and continued speaking, examining her blood-red nails for chips as she spoke.

"You know, Amanda, Jessica Walker and Linda Scott have been telling me how much Samantha and Tyler miss seeing you since you began working at that cable station and started hanging around with your . . . new friends," Mrs. Townsend said.

Amanda ignored her mother's subtle disdain for Keera Johnson and Jamar Williams, her friends and co-workers at KSS-TV.

"Why don't you come with me to the Club today, and you can go sailing with Samantha and Tyler?" Mrs. Townsend suggested hopefully.

"Oh, Mother, I told you last night, when Keera was over and we were doing her hair, that we have to go in to work today. Don't you remember? Drew Pearson, the station manager, called an emergency meeting about —" Amanda began to say.

"Oh, yes, I suppose you did say something about an emergency meeting, although I can't imagine what could be so important that it wouldn't wait until Monday," Mrs. Townsend responded.

"Besides, Hero and I—" Amanda began.

"Oh, Hero," Mrs. Townsend interrupted.

"Yes, Hero," Amanda said stubbornly, sticking out her chin.

"You know, Amanda, you don't really

know anything about that boy at all. We've never met his parents, we don't know where they're from, why they came to Cliffside, or anything," Mrs. Townsend chided her.

Amanda refused to listen to her mother on the subject of Hero. She knew her mother couldn't possibly understand how she and Hero felt about each other. After all, what did her mother know about being in love? Amanda's mother and father hardly saw each other anymore. Amanda couldn't imagine going for even one day without seeing Hero.

Seeing the determination in Amanda's eyes, Mrs. Townsend changed the subject. "Well, if you're not coming to the Club with me, I've got to fly, or we'll get bumped from the air-conditioned court." She turned away from Amanda and headed for the stairs, then paused.

"It wouldn't hurt to spend more time with Samantha and Tyler, like you used to, would it, dear?" Mrs. Townsend called casually over her shoulder.

"And, Amanda, don't forget. Your father's back in town tonight, and we're all going out for a late dinner at the Club.

Be home and ready to go no later than 8:30." Mrs. Townsend's voice wafted up the stairs as the door closed behind her.

Amanda glared after her mother. There was no point in mentioning that this was her one-month anniversary with Hero and that maybe she had other plans. Amanda knew her mother wouldn't care.

Amanda tried to remember a time when she and her mother could really talk to each other, when her mother had really listened to the things that were important to Amanda. But try as she might, Amanda couldn't remember a single situation. Her mother was always busy with the Club and her friends, or the Club and fixing up the house, or just the Club.

Amanda's father was the one who had always taken the time to listen to Amanda. But, after his last big promotion and their move to the "mausoleum," as Amanda referred to their new house, Mr. Townsend had started traveling most of the time. Amanda missed talking to her father. She missed confiding in him.

Amanda would have liked to have told her father about how hateful Tyler had been on the Fourth, and how confused she was by Tyler's ability to pretend that nothing out of the ordinary had happened that night.

And Amanda wanted to talk over how strangely Samantha was behaving— Samantha, who had been her best friend forever!

But her father's quick phone conversations from Japan or England in the middle of the night didn't seem like the right time to bring any of this up. At least he was coming back tonight. Maybe he'd be staying awhile and she'd have a chance to talk with him.

Amanda was so lonely, she almost missed her thirteen-year-old sister, Kit, who was away at sleepaway camp till the middle of the week. Even though they were total opposites, the one thing that held them together was their determination not to be anything like their mother. Amanda would have welcomed a friendly face in the house, even if it was Kit's pesky one.

The roar of an approaching motorcycle broke into Amanda's thoughts. Hero usually picked her up in his mother's old Buick. He preferred that to driving in

Amanda's brand-new white Mustang convertible. Amanda wasn't quite sure why, but she realized it had something to do with his pride. Amanda shrugged off the difference in their financial backgrounds, but it mattered a great deal to Hero.

An undercurrent of excitement had been in Hero's voice last night on the phone when he told her that his cycle might be ready to roll today. How perfect, Amanda thought. My first time on the motorcycle will be on our one-month anniversary. Amanda raced down the stairs and out into the steamy, hot morning.

When Hero saw Amanda looking cool and fresh as she waited for him in front of her house, his heart jumped into his mouth. He couldn't get used to the fact that Amanda Townsend, the prettiest, most popular girl at Cliffside High, was as in love with him as he was with her.

When he'd moved to Cliffside four months ago, Hero hadn't known a soul. He'd been the outsider, always watching from the fringes of every crowd. That's when he'd first noticed Amanda, always at the center of a bunch of admirers, always laughing, tossing her beautiful blonde hair over her shoulder. Back then, all Hero could do was dream about being with Amanda.

But working at KSS-TV this summer had changed all that. Now Hero had good friends, like Jamar and Keera. And, of course, Hero had Amanda, whom he loved more than he thought it was possible to love anyone.

Hero smiled at the memory of that first day, six weeks ago, when Amanda had nearly run him over in her rush to get to the KSS-TV cable station. Hero couldn't believe his good luck when he discovered that they would both be working at the station for the summer.

A shadow crossed his eyes beneath the darkened visor of his helmet. They almost hadn't gotten together, Hero reminded himself. Between Amanda's major crush on Drew early that summer and Tyler's jealous interfering, it was a miracle that Hero and Amanda had managed to work out things between them.

Hero drove up with a flourish, stopping precisely in front of Amanda. Raising his visor, Hero leaned forward to give Amanda a quick kiss on the lips in greeting.

"Hey, beautiful, going my way?" Hero asked jokingly, jumping off the motorcycle to improve on the kiss.

"Oh, Hero, I'm so glad you finally fixed your bike. It looks terrific. In fact, it looks even better than it did before the accident," Amanda told him.

Hero knew that he'd done a good job repairing the '66 FLH, which had been badly damaged in the motorcycle race against Tyler down Cliff Point Road at the July Fourth Beach Bash. It had taken half of his pay from the TV station, and a lot of time working with his father. But the time and money had paid off. Hero was proud of the fact that the cycle was as good as it had ever been.

Hero reached down beneath the saddlebag and handed Amanda a carefully wrapped present. "I was going to save this for later, but I think it's something you'll be needing right away," he said. "Happy anniversary, Amanda."

"Oh, Hero, I didn't get you a present, I mean . . ." Amanda began to say, holding the box uncertainly.

"You've already given me my present," Hero answered simply, looking into Amanda's eyes.

Amanda put the box down and wrapped her arms around Hero's neck. Hero folded her body into his, giving her a long, deep kiss, fusing his lips to hers, holding her as if he would never, ever let her go.

Amanda stepped back and caught her breath. Hero was so intense, it sometimes overwhelmed her.

Hero bent down and picked up the box again. "Aren't you going to open this?" he asked.

Amanda tore at the wrappings and uncovered a motorcycle helmet that was a smaller version of Hero's, with her name printed neatly on the custom-made satin interior.

Although it wasn't exactly the present of Amanda's dreams, she knew this helmet had been expensive. And she also knew how much Hero's motorcycle meant to him. It was as though he had offered her the key to his heart.

Amanda's eyes shone at the gesture. Awkwardly she placed the helmet on her head. Hero reached over and straightened it for her, fastening the strap tightly across her chin.

"Now, my lady, your chariot awaits," Hero said formally, presenting his arm for Amanda to take.

Laughing, Amanda allowed Hero to help her onto the cycle. Then he climbed in front of her.

"What do I do now?" Amanda asked, her voice muffled by the visor as she sat stiffly behind Hero.

"Just hold on tight, and I'll do all the rest," Hero responded, taking Amanda's arms and placing them snugly around his waist. Amanda molded her body against Hero's back. Their bodies fit together perfectly.

Hero's back was warm, and his T-shirt clung to his well-developed muscles. Amanda could feel his lean, hard stomach beneath her fingers. If my mother could see me now, she'd have a fit, Amanda thought delightedly.

Hero gunned the engine and they rocketed off down the street toward the KSS-TV cable station. With the warm wind tearing through her clothes and their bodies moving in sync as they swerved through the Cliffside streets, Amanda felt like she was flying. She could hardly remember why they were on their way to KSS-TV.

Riding on a motorcycle was the most wonderful feeling in the world. No wonder Hero loved it so. Merely driving through the familiar Cliffside streets felt like setting out for an unknown adventure in a faraway place. Contentedly leaning her cheek against Hero's strong back, Amanda felt sure that her love for Hero would last forever.

Keera Johnson pulled up in front of Jamar Williams's house, her mother's ancient station wagon coming to a grinding halt.

Automatically, Keera reached to push up her glasses on her nose, forgetting that she was wearing her brand-new contact lenses. Paying for them had taken a large chunk of her summer earnings, but Keera and Amanda had both agreed that it was worth it. Amanda assured Keera that her new look was guaranteed to make Jamar sit up and take notice.

Keera glanced briefly in the rearview mirror, surprised at her reflection once again. She still wasn't used to seeing herself without her wire-rimmed glasses and with the new hairdo that she and Amanda had worked up last night.

Keera wasn't sure she liked this new hairstyle. Amanda had given Keera a home perm with a kit Amanda had found while she was researching her last story on hairstyles. The soft curling ringlets that fell around Keera's face accentuated her sea-green eyes.

Keera had to admit, she did look very nice, especially with a touch of makeup on her eyes and lips. "Once he sees you, Jamar will totally forget about Rogue Jelsen and the JellyJam band and want to spend every minute with you!" Amanda had told her.

But, staring at the stranger reflected in the rearview mirror, Keera wasn't so sure. When Keera had gotten home last night, her mother had examined Keera closely. She seemed to like the new hairdo, but she wasn't crazy about the makeup.

"You know, Keera, how you look isn't what matters," Mrs. Johnson had told her.

"It's the kind of person you are inside, taking pride in your work and doing well in school and on those SATs. That's what really counts, honey, not fooling around with your hair and your eyes."

Parents, Keera sighed. Here she was, growing up before their eyes, and they treated her like a kid playing dress up.

Keera got out of the car and went to knock on Jamar's door. Then she hesitated.

What if he hates it? Keera worried. What if he thinks I look like a total fool?

She remembered how Jamar would tenderly remove her glasses before kissing her and lovingly stroke her long, straight hair, sending chills all through her body.

Don't be ridiculous, Keera scolded herself. Jamar's so wrapped up in his music and his band, he probably won't even notice. I'll bet he doesn't even remember it's our one-month anniversary.

It was hard to believe it was only a month ago that Keera and Jamar had finally realized their love. The memory of standing in the moonlight, the ocean breeze washing over them, the last of the fireworks flickering in the night sky as Jamar caressed her hair, her cheeks, his

lips murmuring how much he loved her—
it seemed like it was only yesterday.

When their mouths finally joined in one
long kiss, it was as if they were both
parched from thirst and drinking from the
same cool, deep well. Keera had never
been kissed like that before, and she
swooned a bit at the memory.

Since that night, Jamar had been so
busy writing music and rehearsing and
performing with his band that they hadn't
been able to spend as much time together
as Keera would have liked.

Just then, the door opened, and Jamar
shouted, "I'm out of here. I'll wait for
Keera outside—"

Quickly closing the door behind him,
Jamar almost fell over Keera waiting on
the porch.

"Hey, Keera, I'm sorry, I—" Jamar
began. Then he looked at Keera, who was
brushing her curly ringlets out of her eyes.

With a low whistle, Jamar said, "Keera,
girl, what happened to you?"

Blushing, Keera asked, "Do you like it?"

Standing back for a second, Jamar
stared intently at Keera's face.

"Well," he hesitated, "you look . . ."

Keera bit her lip, waiting, saying uncertainly, "I look what . . . ?"

Jamar didn't answer, but his face split into a wide grin. His eyes crinkled at the corners as always, and he grabbed Keera in a bear hug and kissed her full on the mouth.

Noticing Mrs. Williams and Jamar's half sister Jolie staring out at them through the front window, Keera blushed. Giggling self-consciously, she pulled away and ran off toward her mother's car, ducking into the front seat.

"You look great," Jamar called after her, his lean, strong legs striding easily to catch up. He flung himself into the front seat of the car.

As soon as Keera started up the engine, Jamar flipped on the air conditioner and the radio. He fiddled with the buttons until he found the station he wanted. Music filled the car. Jamar leaned back against the worn vinyl seats of Mrs. Johnson's station wagon, basking in the cool air, and closed his eyes.

"Do you really think so?" Keera shouted, trying to be heard over the air conditioner and the radio.

"Think what?" Jamar replied, head bobbing to the music.

"That I look okay," Keera said.

Opening his eyes, Jamar put his hand lightly on Keera's arm. "Definitely," he answered.

Keera sighed. Sometimes she wished Jamar was more like he'd been in the beginning—more interested in her instead of his music.

"So what's this emergency meeting all about?" Jamar asked. "I couldn't really ask Drew any questions, 'cause Jolie and my mom were fighting pretty loud last night."

"What's up with them?" Keera asked sympathetically.

"Aw, who knows?" Jamar shrugged it off. "With me off with the band, working at the station, and spending time with you, I'm not home enough to find out."

And he spends precious little time with me, that's for sure, Keera thought sulkily.

"So, what about Drew?" Jamar asked insistently.

"All he told me was that KSS was having some money problems, and we needed to come in and talk about the programming," Keera answered.

"You think we'll lose our jobs?" Jamar asked worriedly. "I was really counting on the cash for the next three weeks," he added.

Losing her job hadn't occurred to Keera before. Last night when Drew had called, she and Amanda had been so busy doing Keera's hair, they hadn't given Drew's message much thought.

"I hope not," Keera said. Keera's heart sank as she remembered how Drew had explained after their first show that some of the local corporate sponsors might be angry about Keera's hard-hitting segment on how local companies were ruining the Cliffside Lagoon. If the show was in trouble, was it her fault?

Hero and Amanda, on Hero's motorcycle, roared up to the curb just as Keera carefully pulled up in her mother's car. Jamar bounded out of the car, with Keera following close behind him.

"Hey, dude! You fixed it. The cycle looks dynamite," Jamar called to Hero.

"Great helmet, Amanda," Keera said, watching Amanda deftly undo the chin strap. "You look like you were born to ride. How was your first time?"

"It was wonderful," Amanda said excitedly, her eyes sparkling. "Hero has to take you for a ride, Keera. You'd love it."

"Oh, Hero has taken me," Keera said.

"Really? When?" Amanda asked.

Before Keera could answer, Amanda noted Drew's forest-green Saab already parked in front of the station.

"Uh-oh," Amanda said, pointing the car out to Hero and Jamar. "Drew's here before us—for the first time ever, and on a Saturday, no less. Something must really be up."

"Only one way to find out," Hero said. "Let's go in."

Chapter Two

*W*hen Amanda walked into the station, she didn't even notice the cracked flooring, uneven ceiling tiles, and glaring fluorescent lighting that made the KSS-TV cable station look about as unglamorous as a chiropractor's office.

Instead, she focused her attention on Drew Pearson, the handsome twenty-six-year-old station manager, who had persistently lobbied the corporate powers-that-be in Cliffside to fund the summer student programming jobs at the station. Drew was sitting at his desk, head in his hands. A single sheet of paper, which had been crumpled, smoothed out, and recrumpled many times, lay before him on his desk.

Through the plate-glass window walls of his office, Amanda could see that Drew looked tired and harried—quite a contrast from the happy-go-lucky Drew she had met in the beginning of the summer.

During those first couple of weeks at KSS, Amanda had thought she was in love with Drew. He'd been so caring, so attentive, Amanda had been sure there was something between them. But she'd been totally wrong. Amanda still winced at the memory of the night of the Beach Bash, when she met Zoe, Drew's fianceé—and learned that Amanda reminded Drew of his kid sister. *That* was why he had been so kind to Amanda.

It was only then, as if a veil had been lifted from her eyes, that Amanda was able to really see Hero—and see that he had loved her since the moment they met. He had done a pretty good job of hiding his feelings with his flippant remarks and casual sarcasm.

Drew looked up then and spotted his student programmers waiting uncertainly in the hallway. He smiled and waved them all into his office, indicating they should sit on the couch.

"Hey, folks, thanks for coming in on a Saturday. I know how hard you've been working to get the show out each week, and I'm so proud of you all, I just want you to know . . ." Drew paused for a moment, not sure exactly what to say or how to go on.

Hero and Amanda gave each other a worried glance. "Drew, what is it?" Amanda asked with concern.

Taking a deep breath, Drew replied, "It seems the money-well for the student-run programming has suddenly run dry. Essentially, someone's pulled the plug on our funding."

"But who?" Amanda asked in amazement. "Our show is a hit. Everyone loves us."

"I'm not sure who," he answered.

"But why?" Keera asked.

"I've been told that it's because some people feel the reporting is too amateurish, and they want their money to go toward something more adult," Drew said, indicating the crumpled letter on his desk. "But, truthfully, I don't believe this 'amateurish' claim is the real reason. Your spoofs are great, and your investigative reports are as professional as they come," Drew assured them. "I intend to get the scoop on this. But, for now . . . "

Drew stopped and took a deep breath. "Student KSS is off the air, effective as of next week's show. Unless . . ."

"Unless . . . what?" Jamar asked unhappily, already trying to figure out where he was going to get another job three weeks before school started.

"Well," Drew spoke slowly, an idea beginning to take shape behind his eyes, "unless we can find another way to fund the show."

"How are we supposed to do that?" Hero asked.

Looking around at the sad and hopeless expressions on everyone's faces, Amanda said, "Maybe we could raise our own money to do the show."

Jamar, Keera, and Hero looked at Amanda as though she'd spoken in an alien tongue. Where were they going to get that kind of money? Amanda's parents might have the money to kick in for her segment, but no one else was in the same position.

Realizing that she wasn't making herself understood, Amanda cleared her throat and started again.

"I mean, maybe we could have some

kind of fund raiser, like a telethon, or a marathon, or something. I just know if the kids in Cliffside heard that our show was being canceled, they'd come out in droves to help keep us on the air," Amanda said. Her cheeks flushed brightly, her big violet eyes dancing in the light.

Catching Amanda's enthusiasm, Jamar jumped in. "Why don't we have a fund-raiser concert?" he suggested.

"You mean, use the last show's air time to pull in funds to keep the programming going?" Drew said. "We could set up a computerized hot line for ticket sales and contributions . . ."

"And we could broadcast the concert live, outdoors, maybe at Cliffside Park. We can bill it as the coolest event of the summer—the first, live Cliffside KSS-TV concert," Hero said, getting caught up in the excitement.

"We can call it the KSS-Off Concert," Amanda added. "That way everyone will understand that, without the money from this concert, we're doomed."

"But who are we going to get to play for the concert that everyone would be willing to pay to see?" Keera asked quietly.

"Well, there's always JellyJam," Jamar said quickly.

"Of course, dude," Hero said, "but Keera's got a point. We've got to have more than just one act to make a fundraising concert."

Everyone sat around, thinking hard.

Then Drew cleared his throat. "I just might be able to make a few calls and get some celebrity rock groups to show up," he said slowly. "If it all works out, we could have the concert next Saturday."

Everyone looked at Drew in surprise. They hadn't really thought of him as being well-connected in the rock world.

Drew laughed at the expressions on their faces. "I guess I never mentioned to you folks what Zoe does," he said.

"Enlighten us, fearless leader," Hero joked.

"Zoe is the associate producer for Rock America on HIP-TV."

"She is?" Amanda asked in disbelief. Then she remembered that, at the beginning of the summer, Drew had mentioned he attended the Grammy Awards every year. Now she realized why.

Jamar let out a low whistle. This was just the kind of break he and Rogue had been dreaming about. With great ceremony, Jamar stood up, walked over to Drew's desk, and handed him the telephone.

"By all means, my man, call your lady," Jamar urged.

Drew reached for the telephone.

They all watched Drew's face intently, listening while he explained the funding problems and concert suggestion to Zoe. After a few excruciating minutes, Drew's face broke out into a wide grin, and he gave them all a thumbs up.

Hanging up the phone, Drew told them, "Zoe said she'll make some calls, talk up the concert, and see who's going to be in town next week to do it. We'll know by the end of today whom she'll be able to line up for us."

"All right!" Jamar said. He slapped Drew and Hero five and started moonwalking around the room.

Amanda smiled at Jamar's antics. Maybe it was going to be all right after all.

"Uh, Drew, *if* we do get some celebrities —" Keera began.

"You mean *when*, girl. Say *when*," Jamar scolded her.

"I mean *when* we get the celebrities," Keera said, grinning at Jamar, "do you really think we'll be able to pull it off by next week?"

"Of course we will," Jamar said. "We're going to rock Cliffside right into the ocean."

"Well, realistically, a week isn't much time," Drew said with a sigh.

Amanda was lost in thought. Hero reached over and lightly stroked the tiny crinkle between her eyebrows.

"What's your plan, Amanda?" Hero asked gently. "I can tell you've got something cooking up there."

"Well, I just think that, in order to do the concert right, in one week, we're going to need some help," Amanda said.

"That's true, what with the publicity, getting the tickets printed, putting together the equipment, setting up the bandstand, managing the stage, taping the show, manning the phones . . ." Drew's voice trailed off, as he saw the somewhat daunted look on everyone's face.

All at once, Amanda's face brightened. Hero watched with wonder as sparks caught in Amanda's eyes and her cheeks flushed slightly.

"I have the perfect plan," Amanda said excitedly. "I know that all the kids in town will be crushed if our program goes off the air. I bet *they'd* volunteer to help with the concert. Let's run a tickertape prompt all day today on the station, calling for volunteers. The phones will be ringing off the hook by Monday," Amanda assured them.

"Oh, I wouldn't be so sure about that, Amanda," Hero said skeptically. "Everyone who needs a job is already hooked for the summer."

"Well, I know a lot of my friends aren't working, and maybe they'd help if we asked them," Amanda suggested.

"Oh, come on, Amanda. Your friends are probably too busy yachting or wind-surfing to do any real work," Hero said. Besides, he thought to himself, who wants them around here anyway?

Amanda's face flushed a deep red. She had almost forgotten how Hero could go from sweet to sarcastic in the blink of an eye. In a flash she remembered how Hero had made fun of her the first day they met, when she told him she wanted to work at KSS because she was tired of hanging around the yacht club.

Before Amanda could reply, Jamar interrupted them.

"Yo, Hero. I say, let's give Amanda's idea a try!"

"I agree," Drew said with an encouraging smile at Amanda.

Amanda smiled brightly in return, determined to ignore Hero's cynicism.

Seeing the determined look on Amanda's face, Keera decided to offer her support. "Really, Hero, what have we got to lose?" Keera asked, giving Amanda a quick smile.

But, secretly, Keera agreed with Hero. She couldn't imagine Samantha Walker or Tyler Scott rolling up their sleeves and getting down to work, especially to help out at KSS. It was true that Amanda wasn't like the group of snobs she hung out with at Cliffside High. But Samantha and Tyler were another story.

Could they really be capable of volunteering to help anyone? Not likely, Keera thought to herself. And we'll all be better off if they don't.

Chapter Three

"Okay, people, let's see what we can accomplish today to get this thing going," Drew said, already making lists of things that needed to be done.

Amanda sighed and glanced over at Hero. "Guess this means the picnic lunch is off for today," she said unhappily as they walked out of Drew's office together.

"Maybe, if we get done early enough, we can still make it—for a twilight picnic," Hero suggested softly, taking hold of Amanda's hand. "Watching the sun set, listening to the waves . . ." Hero thought this sounded even better than the afternoon plan.

Amanda was caught up in the romance of Hero's description. She could already see herself snuggling into his arms, leaning against his muscled chest, as they sat on the grassy bluff in the waning light—the sky melting into streaks of orange, then purple, then blue. The perfect anniversary celebration.

Amanda looked directly at Hero, imagining that they were on the bluff. The fluorescent lighting, crooked ceiling tiles, and cracked flooring fell away. Amanda longed for Hero to take her in his arms and crush his mouth to hers.

"Excuse me, pardon me," Jamar said mockingly, interrupting Amanda and Hero's conversation as he tried to get past them to his desk.

Amanda blushed and sat down in her chair.

"Give me a break, dude," Hero said, giving Jamar a jab on the shoulder. Then he leaned against the edge of Amanda's desk.

Keera stepped beside Hero, clipboard in hand, pen at the ready—the epitome of businesslike efficiency.

"I've jotted down a few notes from our meeting with Drew, and here's where we need to begin," she said. "First we need to get someone to donate bandstand equipment, amps, wires, and a bigger sound system than we've got at the station."

"That job's got Amanda's name all over it," Jamar said with a grin. "After doing that 'Short Cuts' show on haircuts—and seeing how people will mutate their heads just to be on Amanda's spot—Amanda could talk an elephant through a keyhole."

"Thanks a lot, Jam," Amanda said wryly, twisting her lips into a half-smile, half-frown.

What does that mean? Keera wondered to herself, unconsciously touching her own newly curled hair. Does Jamar think I look as ridiculous as the people did on Amanda's show? Her eyes stung at the thought, and it took a moment for her to get back into the work mode.

Hero, seeing Keera touch her newly permed hair, realized that her feelings had been hurt. Reaching out to gently touch her arm, Hero said with great chivalry, "And what, lovely lady, would you have me do?"

Flashing Hero a grateful look, Keera continued, "Well, we need to get the concert tickets printed, establish a box office, and set up a hotline on the computer for taking in the money."

"Sounds like a task for cyberdork, my alter ego," Hero offered. He'd set his mind to conquering his distaste for computers this summer, and he had been the only one to work with Drew on the computer on the programming budget and financial matters.

"Great," Keera said, smiling, as she tried to envision Hero as a cyberdork.

Hero moved toward the computer to get started.

"Coordinating the music, entertainment, and concessions," Keera read from her list. She looked expectantly toward Jamar.

"Soon as Drew tells me who we've got, I'm there," Jamar said. "If you promise to help me with the food stuff, that is," he added. "Meanwhile, I'll just telephone my JellyJam brothers and let them know the happy news, so we can start planning our musical strategy. We can deal with the concessions stuff later on."

"Keera, don't forget about the ticker-tape prompt asking for volunteers," Amanda piped up.

"Sure," Keera said. "I'll take care of that while I'm working up the flyers and press releases to the other cable stations. We can plug in the names of the groups who'll be performing when we know who they are, and then maybe you guys could help me distribute them," Keera said, busily scribbling. She wondered how she was ever going to get everything done for the concert, help Jamar, and study nights, too.

After working most of the day without even stopping for a break to eat, Amanda and the others were exhausted.

Every time Drew's phone line lit up, they had all hoped it would be Zoe, telling them who would be willing to play at the concert. But, each time, Drew shook his head.

Drew had spent most of the day on the phone, trying to track down the source of the funds cutoff, but he hadn't been very successful. Whoever had pulled the plug was pretty intent about not being found.

Wearily rising from his desk, Drew walked over to the doorway of his office and said, "Okay, crew, I think it's time for you to wrap it up for today. I just have a few more calls to make. I'll talk to Zoe tonight and see what she has to say. Then we can pick it up again on Monday."

Amanda stretched her arms over her head, trying to get the crick out of her neck. She sighed with weary triumph. She had spent hours convincing Cliffside Edison to supply a couple of auxiliary generators for power, Cliffside Electric to supply the lighting, and Cliffside Electronics to donate the speakers and amps, along with a couple of workers to set up the speakers and work the lighting for the concert as well.

Hero came up behind her, and she felt his strong, warm hand circle her neck. He rubbed his thumb along the exact spot that hurt. Amanda leaned back and gazed up into Hero's eyes. The pressure of his strong, lean fingers working into her neck felt divine.

"Drew's right, guys," Hero said, stifling a yawn. "I'm done for."

"Just one more second. I'm almost finished," Keera said, pressing the "Save" button on her computer. Then she went over to Jamar, who was still on the phone, and snuggled up against him.

"Time to go," Keera mouthed. Jamar grinned, said, "Later, man!" and hung up.

Pulling Jamar out of his seat, Keera said

42

impetuously, "Come on, Jamar. Let's go do something fun, like walk on the beach or see a movie."

Jamar groaned.

"Aw, Keera, I can't," Jamar explained. "Rogue thinks the band needs some serious rehearsing tonight to figure out what we're going to play at the concert. I'll see you tomorrow, and we'll make all those concession stand calls together, like you promised, okay?"

Keera let Jamar's hand drop from her grasp, biting back her disappointment. She had been willing to give up one night of studying. The least Jamar could have done was give up a night's rehearsal, Keera thought.

As they all headed for the door, calling their good-byes to Drew, Jamar added sweetly, "Keera, I told Rogue you'd drop me off at his house. Okay with you, girlfriend?"

For the past month it had been Rogue this, Rogue that. It was a wonder Jamar could use the bathroom without Rogue's permission, Keera thought nastily. Now it was their one-month anniversary, and Jamar hadn't even so much as said a word about it.

"What if it isn't?" Keera asked.

Looking at her in surprise, Jamar said, "Say what?"

"I said, what if it isn't okay with me?" Keera repeated.

"What's the problem?" Jamar asked evenly, not wanting to get into a discussion about Rogue and the boys. He had enough nagging from his mother and sister. He wasn't about to start taking it from Keera, too.

"Nothing, just forget it. But you're not the only one with other things to do, you know," Keera muttered. She could hear her mother's voice echoing in her head, lecturing her about spending time mooning over a no-good musician instead of studying and preparing for the SATs this fall.

Holding up his hands in surrender, Jamar said, "Okay, girl. I don't know what's up with you, but, if that's the way you want it, fine. I'll find my own way to Rogue's."

And with that, Jamar went back inside the station, without a single glance backward.

Stunned that Jamar would walk away

from her like that, Keera numbly walked over to her car, mechanically opened the door, and sat staring unseeingly at the steering wheel. Score one for Rogue, she thought unhappily to herself.

Hero's arm was draped possessively around Amanda's shoulders as they walked down the path to the street.

"How about that twilight picnic?" Hero whispered into Amanda's gleaming blonde hair.

Leaning her head against Hero's shoulder, Amanda closed her eyes, allowing the vision of the two of them alone on the bluff in the moonlight to wash over her.

Then, with a start, Amanda remembered her mother's dinner plans for this evening. "Oh, Hero, I can't."

Stiffening slightly, Hero asked, "How come?"

"It's my dad's first night back in town after three weeks of traveling. I'm supposed to have dinner with him and my mother," Amanda told him unhappily.

"At the Yacht Club?" Hero asked archly.

"Wait a minute. Why don't you come to

dinner with us?" Amanda asked, her eyes sparkling with excitement.

"Did your mother invite me?" Hero asked slowly.

"Well, no, but it would give you and my parents a chance to get to know one another. And I just know that you and my dad would get along. And my mother— well, we can work on my mother . . ." Amanda's voice trailed off as she saw the hard look on Hero's face.

"This isn't exactly how I'd envisioned today," Hero said quietly.

"I know," Amanda interrupted, "but we can celebrate after the concert next Saturday. I really do have to go to dinner with them tonight, Hero. Won't you come, too?" Amanda asked prettily, tracing her finger along the muscle on Hero's upper arm.

"I really don't think it would be a good idea," Hero said.

"Please?" Amanda begged. "I'm sure it'll be okay with my folks."

Hero could just imagine how Mrs. Townsend would look at him when he drove up to the Club with Amanda on his motorcycle. And he certainly couldn't see himself riding in the family car.

Shaking his head, Hero said stubbornly, "No, Amanda. Maybe some other time."

"I can't believe you're not going to do this for me," Amanda said. "And on our anniversary, too," she added with a sniff.

"You can deal, Amanda. I'm not going," Hero said, pulling on his helmet. "Come on, I'll drop you off at home. We can talk tomorrow." Hero straddled his motorcycle, holding out Amanda's helmet to her.

"Thank you, but I'll find my own way home," Amanda said stiffly.

"Amanda—" Hero began impatiently.

"I'm not kidding. See you around, Hero," Amanda said, walking off.

"If that's the way you want it," Hero said with a shrug. He flipped down his visor so Amanda couldn't see the hurt in his eyes, gunned the engine, and roared off, leaving Amanda's helmet sitting on the sidewalk.

Amanda was astonished. She turned around and watched as Hero's cycle zoomed off into the distance. Numbly, she walked over to the sidewalk, knelt down, and picked up the helmet. Surely Hero would turn around and come back for her.

But after several long minutes of

straining to hear the whine of Hero's cycle, Amanda finally had to admit defeat.

Amanda's face colored and her eyes flashed. How dare Hero leave her standing on the sidewalk like this, no matter what she said!

It was clear that Amanda was going to have to figure out some other mode of transportation. It was much too far to walk home. Amanda cringed at the possibility of having to call her mother.

Just then, Amanda noticed Keera sitting behind the wheel of her mother's car, alone, not going anywhere.

Amanda rapped on the passenger-side window, then quickly opened the door and sat down beside her friend.

"What are you still doing here? I thought you and Hero were going out for your anniversary," Keera asked with a tinge of bitterness in her voice.

"Where's Jamar?" Amanda countered, not wanting to talk about Hero right then.

"He's inside the station, calling . . . calling . . . Rogue," Keera said faintly, her eyes blinking back the tears.

"Oh," Amanda said quietly and looked down at the helmet in her hands.

"Where's Hero?" Keera asked again, more gently this time.

"Oh, he roared off into the sunset, alone, in a huff," Amanda said in a quavering voice.

Keera looked hard at Amanda. Then, as if snapping out of a trance, she felt moved to action.

"So, how about if I drive you home then?" Keera asked matter-of-factly, starting up the car.

"What about Jamar? Shouldn't we wait for him?" Amanda asked.

"Jamar?" Keera asked, as if Amanda had suddenly started speaking Swahili.

"Yeah, Jamar, you know, the cute musician, the one you've been dating for a month—" Amanda said teasingly.

"Oh, yes, I vaguely remember him," Keera said with a tremulous smile. "I believe Jamar is making other travel arrangements, even as we speak. And I'm not so sure we're still dating," Keera added, her eyes once again filling with tears.

"Really?" Amanda asked.

"Really," Keera said firmly, her sea-green eyes focusing straight ahead on the traffic ahead of her. "After all, I've got college to think about, SATs to study for. I don't have time to hang around waiting for Jamar between sets."

"I thought I was the only one having trouble," Amanda murmured. "Want to talk about it?"

Keera nodded. A tear slipped down her cheek.

Chapter Four

Keera pulled her mother's car up in front of Amanda's house.

"What are we going to do about these guys?" Amanda asked, not really expecting an answer.

"Who knows? I should probably spend more time hitting the books than I do waiting around for Jamar anyway," Keera responded with a shrug.

"Well, don't study too hard, Keera. And thanks for listening," Amanda said with a teary smile.

"You, too," Keera told her.

Amanda reached over and gave Keera a quick hug. "I'm so glad we're friends," Amanda whispered shyly.

Brushing the last remnants of tears from her face, Amanda took a deep breath and headed for the door. Glancing at her watch, she realized it was already 7:30.

She only had an hour to get ready before dinner.

Rushing up the wide carpeted steps, Amanda called out, "I'm home!"

"We're up here, princess." Mr. Townsend's voice rang out from the master bedroom, where he and Mrs. Townsend were getting dressed for dinner.

"Dad!" Amanda shouted excitedly, taking the remaining steps two at a time as she raced toward the bedroom.

Mr. Townsend seemed a little tired. But he was the same distinguished and handsome father she knew and loved, especially in the elegant silk suit he was wearing for tonight's dinner. Mrs. Townsend was her usual beautiful self in a sleeveless cream-colored linen dress, ivory pumps, and a touch of pearls at the neck and ears.

They look like grown-up Barbie and Ken dolls, Amanda thought briefly. Then she dashed into the room, almost knocking over her mother in order to give her father a big bear hug.

"Oh, Daddy, I'm so glad you're home," Amanda said warmly.

"I'm glad to be home, princess. This

was a long, hard trip. Too long," Mr. Townsend said, hugging Amanda tightly.

"So, what have you been doing, Amanda?" her father asked affably, standing back to take a good look at her. "I'd swear you've grown. Something's different about you," Mr. Townsend said.

"Oh, Amanda thinks she's in love," Mrs. Townsend replied.

Amanda looked daggers at her mother. Leave it to her to say something like that!

"My little girl, in love? How did this happen? Who's the lucky guy? Is he joining us for dinner?" Mr. Townsend asked.

"No, he's not," Amanda said, shaking her head and trying not to cry.

"What's the matter, sweetheart?" Mr. Townsend asked with concern, pulling Amanda close.

Tossing back her head, Amanda said with forced brightness, "Nothing's wrong, really. Everything's perfect."

"Isn't it time you got dressed, Amanda? I left a dress on your bed. I picked it up for you today. Our reservation is for 8:45, and you know how the Club hates it when we're late," Mrs. Townsend remarked.

Giving her dad another quick hug, Amanda slipped out of her parents' room and into her own. She wasn't going to let her tears over Hero spoil her dad's first night home. She was determined to make the evening a happy one.

Amanda and her parents entered the spacious, glassed-in dining room of the Cliffside Yacht Club. The elaborately set tables, covered with heavy linen tablecloths, were almost all occupied. The room hummed with conversation and laughter, amidst the tinkling of glasses and the clatter of silverware and china. The fragrance of steamed clams, lobster bisque, and shrimp lingered in the air.

The host graciously greeted the Townsends as old friends and showed them to a large corner table that looked out on the stunning view of the ocean.

For a moment, Amanda imagined Hero walking into the dining room with her family. Looking at it all through his eyes, Amanda could understand why Hero hadn't wanted to join them. But that was no excuse for leaving her on the street, Amanda thought to herself.

"Penny for your thoughts, Amanda," Mr. Townsend said in a gently teasing voice.

Amanda looked into her father's kind blue eyes. She was thinking that she just might tell him about Hero and their first real fight, when Mrs. Townsend said in a cheery voice, "Oh, Harrison, look—the Scotts and the Walkers are here. Why don't we ask them to join us?" Without waiting for a reply, Mrs. Townsend motioned to the arriving couples, who smiled agreeably and headed toward the Townsend table.

"Oh, and look, Amanda. Samantha and Tyler are here, too. What a wonderful opportunity for us all to get together again," Mrs. Townsend said brightly.

Amanda looked over at her mother, suspicious that she had set this whole dinner up. But Mrs. Townsend was the picture of wide-eyed innocence.

"Hello, Samantha. Hello, Tyler," Amanda said in a guarded voice as they approached the table.

"Amanda!" Samantha crowed with delight. But Tyler's face momentarily darkened at the sight of Amanda. He wasn't about to forgive her for choosing Hero that night of the Beach Bash.

"Hey, Amanda," Tyler said stiffly.

"Tyler, my boy, is that any way to greet one of the loveliest females in the room?" Mr. Scott's voice boomed reprovingly as he bent to give Amanda a huge hug. Amanda blushed deeply at Mr. Scott's remark.

After the interminable cheek-kissing ritual was over, everyone settled into seats. Somehow, Tyler ended up sitting beside Amanda, and Samantha was seated across from them both.

"So, Amanda, what have you been up to?" Tyler asked evenly.

"Oh, nothing much. Working on stories for the show, hanging out, that kind of thing," Amanda answered tentatively.

Although Amanda had been friends with Tyler Scott all her life, after the showdown at the Beach Bash between Tyler and Hero, Amanda wasn't sure that she'd ever wanted to speak to Tyler again. But she had to admit, Tyler did look good tonight—his skin smoothly tanned against his crisp white shirt, his sandy-brown hair perfectly in place. And he looked so at home in this room filled with elegance and money.

"That's cool," Tyler said quietly.

Here inside the glass-paned walls of the elegant restaurant, today's crisis at KSS and her argument with Hero seemed like light-years away. Amanda relaxed against the plushly upholstered chair and started to enjoy being back on familiar ground.

After a poke in the ribs from her mother, Samantha spoke up. "So, is everything going okay, with work and everything?"

"Yeah, everything's okay," Amanda said in an unconvincing voice.

"And that cute hunk, Hero, are you and he still together?" Samantha asked innocently.

Amanda's eyes filled for a moment. Then she shook off the tears.

"Yeah, I guess so," Amanda said. She didn't want Tyler or Samantha to know there was anything wrong.

"Is something bothering you, Amanda?" Tyler asked.

"Well, actually," Amanda began, taking a deep breath, "I do have kind of a big problem."

Tyler sat up with sudden interest.

Amanda continued, "We're trying to put together an emergency celebrity concert to save our show, but we've only got a week to do it. I mean, there's only five of us to work on it, if you count Drew, and . . . and . . . I was wondering if maybe you guys . . . might want to . . . help us out?"

Samantha's ears perked up at the word "celebrity." "What kind of concert is this again?" she asked.

"Wait, let me start at the beginning," Amanda said.

Amanda explained the whole situation. Both Tyler and Samantha listened intently, never taking their eyes from Amanda while she spoke.

Seeing Amanda engaged in animated conversation with her friends, Mrs. Townsend allowed herself a satisfied smile. Things were finally getting back to normal.

Chapter Five

"Hey, everyone!" Amanda said cheerily as she entered the KSS station early Monday morning, looking tanned and happy in a cool, white linen shorts outfit. "Whew, it's hot out there again," she added, walking into Drew's office where everyone else was already gathered.

Hero caught his breath at Amanda's appearance. He'd been miserable all day Sunday, waiting for Amanda to call and apologize—but she never had.

"Hey, Amanda, you look great. Where were you yesterday? I called a couple of times, when I was taking a break from studying, but I just kept getting your machine," Keera asked.

"Oh, I'm sorry, Keera. I got back too late to call. I went sailing with my dad yesterday at the Club," Amanda replied breezily, refusing to meet Hero's steady gaze.

"Whatever you did, it sure agreed with you," Drew said, looking at Amanda approvingly. "I hope you all got some rest yesterday, because this week is going to be a killer," he added.

"Did you talk to Zoe? What did she say?" Amanda asked.

"I just got off the phone with her," Drew told them.

"Come on, man, what's the scoop?" Jamar asked impatiently.

"Zoe says that after telling Nick Ganos about the concert—"

"Zoe knows Nick Ganos of Grim Reaper?" Jamar yelled.

"Sssh," Keera said impatiently. Keera hadn't yet forgiven Jamar, and she had refused to come to the phone last night when he called. "She's too busy studying," was the reason her mother gave him.

"Nick Ganos said he and Grim Reaper would love to do the KSS-Off Concert. And his girlfriend, Jamie West of Jezebels, is traveling with Nick next week, and she wants to perform, too," Drew said with a note of triumph in his voice.

"Yes!" Hero said, forgetting to be cool in his excitement.

60

"All right!" Amanda cried. Without thinking, she grabbed Hero and hugged him, forgetting they were mad at each other.

As their skin touched, they both melted. Amanda looked into Hero's eyes, and a smile crept across Hero's mouth. Hero hugged Amanda back, and they stood smiling at each other, all anger forgotten.

"No way!" Keera said in disbelief.

"I'm going to get to play warm-up for Grim Reaper!" Jamar cried, unable to contain himself.

"Okay, now, folks. Don't celebrate too long. As you may recall, we've only got six days, including today, to make this concert a reality," Drew added soberly.

"Hey, I've got a surprise!" Amanda interrupted. "I ran into Tyler and Samantha over the weekend, and I told them all about needing help for the concert and stuff. And guess what?"

"They said they'd come to the concert only if we held it at the Club, so they wouldn't have to get off their yachts," Hero said sarcastically.

"Guess again," Amanda retorted, pulling away from Hero in annoyance.

"They offered to come to work every day

and help out," Keera said, half kidding.

"Right!" Amanda said happily, looking around. Everyone else in the room was quiet.

"Well, good," Drew said. "We'll need all the help we can get. So get going, guys—time's a-wasting."

Hero walked stiffly from the room, crossed the distance to the door, and slammed himself outside. The heat blasted him in the face.

Amanda hesitated a moment, a mixture of anger and hurt on her face, then followed him out the door.

"Hero, I know that you and Tyler don't get along. I mean, I know it's more than not getting along—but Tyler told me he was really sorry about what happened on the beach and he didn't know why he acted so crazy. He seemed so sincere . . ."

Hero whirled around, anger blazing in his dark brown eyes.

"When did he tell you this, at dinner Saturday night—at the Yacht Club?" Hero asked, practically spitting out the words.

Amanda stuck out her chin, her violet eyes crackling with fury. "Yes, as a matter of fact he did!" she replied.

Hero turned away. Despite the blazing

heat, he felt cold. There was an icy pain in his chest, and unwanted tears of disappointment and anger welled up in his throat. Face it, he said to himself. You'll always be the outsider.

"Great. I hope you and your friends and your parents all had a lovely time," Hero replied as coolly as he could.

"Hero, I invited *you* to dinner, but you didn't want to come. Remember?" Amanda pointed out.

Hero's eyes looked like chipped flint.

"Oh, Hero, couldn't we just move on? Tyler and Samantha have been my friends all my life. Our families ran into each other at the Club, by coincidence," Amanda explained. "I just want everyone to be friends. Tyler and Samantha want that, too. Couldn't you try to do that for me? Please?" Amanda said with a soft sigh, lightly stroking Hero's well-muscled arm.

Amanda's fingers were like tiny flames, searing Hero's skin. Heat raced through his blood, melting the coldness that had wrapped itself around his heart.

"I'm sorry about our fight the other day," Amanda continued, slowly moving closer to Hero, until their bodies were practically touching. Hero could almost feel Amanda's silky hair playing against his face.

"Hero?" Amanda said quietly, moving closer. "I won't let anyone or anything come between us," she promised. "I love you."

Looking into Amanda's violet eyes, Hero felt like he was drowning. The blood roared behind his eyes, his heart pounded against his ribs.

Searching Amanda's face, Hero relented. He took her in his arms and pulled her roughly to him.

"I love you, too," Hero whispered fiercely in her hair.

Amanda took Hero's face in her hands and gently pulled his mouth toward hers.

Just then, the station door opened and Jamar poked his head out. Seeing Amanda and Hero, Jamar called back inside, "There's no blood. No one's dead. And they're kissing again!"

Amanda blushed right down to the tips of her toes and made a face at Jamar.

"Well, now that you're back to happily ever after, you guys better get in here so we can move on. We've got a concert to produce," Jamar said.

"Right," Hero said, putting his arm

around Amanda as they walked back into the station, ready to work.

With a lingering last look at Hero, Amanda headed for her desk. Her next assignment was to get local business contributions for the concert in exchange for free advertising. Amanda turned to the "A" section of the Cliffside Yellow Pages.

"Here goes nothing," Amanda said cheerily as she started to dial.

Hero got busy on the computer, setting up the ticketing program.

In a flurry of typing and telephone calls, Keera finished up the press releases, faxed them out to the local stations and papers, and turned to the task of completing the publicity flyers.

Meanwhile, Jamar called food concessions and local restaurants for drink and food donations.

They all were so immersed in what they were doing that, when Tyler and Samantha walked into the station, no one even noticed.

Tyler walked over to Amanda, who was intently studying the D page in the Yellow Pages.

"Earth to Amanda, Earth to Amanda," Tyler said, placing his hands lightly on the back of Amanda's chair.

Flustered, Amanda spun around. She greeted Samantha and Tyler nervously, with a slightly worried look over at Hero. The air was thick with tension.

Then Hero smiled grimly at Tyler and Samantha and said, "Hey" in a low voice.

"How's it going?" Tyler said coolly.

Samantha sauntered over to Hero and gave him a quick peck on the cheek. "Hey, Hero. Good to see you again," she said sweetly.

Color rose on Hero's face, but he stretched his lips into a forced smile and replied, "Yeah, you, too."

At last Amanda was able to let out her breath. She flashed Hero a grateful look.

"So, our first and only volunteers! Let me show you guys around," Amanda said, "before we put you to work."

While Amanda took Samantha and Tyler through the station, Hero sat down heavily at his desk and stared blankly at the papers scattered there.

Keera watched sympathetically from across the room. She knew how much Hero hated Tyler and Samantha—and with good reason. Keera wasn't crazy about them either.

She was just about to say something to

Hero when the station door burst open again. To Keera's total disbelief, there was Rogue in a wild African-design shirt, beads dangling from his neck and ears, dark shades atop his many rows of braids.

"Hey, Keera. Always a pleasure, I can tell," Rogue remarked dryly as she stared at him.

"Rogue, what are you doing here?" Hero asked. "I thought you'd be rehearsing round the clock."

"Well, we need our keyboard man, and he's busy making calls," Rogue said, indicating Jamar, who was deep in conversation at the far side of the office.

When Jamar turned around and saw Rogue in the doorway, he quickly finished up his call. Then he bounced over to greet his best friend.

"Hey, dude, what's shaking?" Jamar said, clasping Rogue's hand in a special grip.

"You said the lovely Keera had given you lots to do this week, and I thought I'd mosey on down to see what I could do to get you out from behind this desk and back on the jammin' track. After all, you can't be spending time doing diddly stuff. We've got to rehearse for this big shindig," Rogue said, looking over at Keera meaningfully.

"Cool. We can use the help," Jamar said enthusiastically. "Keera, what can my man Rogue do?" Jamar asked.

Rogue can go down to the bottom of the ocean for all I care, Keera thought to herself, eyeing Rogue unhappily. Out loud she said, "Well, I suppose he could distribute this pile of flyers I've printed out advertising the concert and the groups."

Rogue examined a flyer critically. "Why is JellyJam listed last?"

"Believe it or not, Rogue, JellyJam isn't the most important thing in the world," Keera snapped. "Getting people to come to the concert—which they will, if they know that Grim Reaper and the Jezebels are coming— is what's important."

"Whoa, slow down, girl," Rogue said. "I was just playing with you."

"Come on, man," Jamar said to Rogue. "I want you to hear some new background stuff I've been fooling with before we get down to work."

Rogue looked over his shoulder and smirked at Keera.

Keera glared back. Round two to Rogue. Keera wondered when it was going to be her turn to win.

Chapter Six

*H*ero looked hard at Keera. She looked about as thrilled that Rogue had shown up as he was about Tyler and Samantha.

"Keera," Hero said in a low voice, not wanting the others to hear. "How about we go for a ride on my cycle, put up the flyers around town, then get something to eat at the Snack Shack?"

Keera looked at Hero in surprise. "What about Amanda? Shouldn't we ask her if she'd like to come?"

"She seems pretty busy to me. I doubt she'll even know we're gone," Hero answered with a grimace, nodding his head in the direction of the visual mixer control room, where Amanda stood laughing with Tyler and Samantha.

"I know what you mean," Keera said, glancing after Jamar and Rogue.

"Come on, let's blow this popsicle

stand." Hero took her firmly by the elbow and moved her toward the door.

Keera smiled. "You sound like Amanda," she teased.

"Really? Well, slap me if I start talking about the Yacht Club." Hero grinned and scooped up the pile of flyers as he and Keera quietly left the station.

Keera confidently straddled the motorcycle seat behind Hero, automatically positioning her body behind his. "Here, you take my helmet," Hero offered gallantly.

"Okay," Keera said, fumbling with the chin strap.

Hero reached back and fastened it for her.

Looking up into Hero's eyes, Keera said softly, "Thanks."

"No problem," Hero replied, letting his hand linger for a moment on Keera's chin.

Suddenly, Keera's eyes filled with tears.

"Cheer up—Rogue's not into a desk job. He'll be history by the time we get back," Hero comforted her.

"I wish he were ancient history," Keera muttered with more venom than she could believe of herself.

"I hear you," Hero said, wishing the same for Tyler and Samantha.

Impulsively, Keera leaned over and gave Hero a quick kiss on the cheek.

Surprised, Hero touched his fingers to his face. Then, embarrassed, he ducked his head, turned, and gunned the engine.

Keera placed her arms around Hero's waist and prepared for takeoff.

Amanda and her friends were heading back to her desk when Tyler noticed the lone computer in a small room off Drew's office. "Who uses that?" Tyler asked with casual interest.

"Oh, Hero and Drew, mainly. That's where Hero's setting up the special funds account from the ticket sales and call-in contributions," Amanda replied.

"Really," Tyler said, his eyes narrowed in thought.

Amanda realized the office was practically empty. "I wonder where Hero and Keera are," Amanda said.

"Yeah, I was really beginning to miss the tension in the room," Tyler joked.

Amanda gave him a warning look.

"Just kidding."

"Well, I think I saw Hero leave with Keera just a minute ago. . ." Samantha said, her voice trailing off.

"Oh," Amanda said. She was surprised that neither Hero nor Keera had said good-bye.

"You can probably still see them out the window," Samantha offered, going over to the window to look. "Yep, they're getting ready to split."

Amanda walked over to the window and peered out. She relaxed when she noticed the pink flyers sticking out from Hero's saddlebag.

"Oh, they must be going out to put up the flyers about the concert," Amanda said matter-of-factly.

She was just about to turn away from the window when Keera kissed Hero and wrapped her arms around his waist.

"I guess Keera and Hero have become really good friends, huh, Amanda?" Samantha asked innocently.

Amanda's stomach felt queasy. Why was Keera kissing Hero? Suddenly she remembered Keera's remark Saturday morning—how Keera had ridden Hero's motorcycle before. Then Amanda shook her head. Don't be ridiculous, she told herself. Hero loves you and Keera's your friend. There must be some other explanation.

"They're just going to post those flyers for the concert," Amanda repeated. "Come on, let's get busy. You guys can use Keera's and Hero's desks. Samantha, you help me by calling the Ls through Qs, and Tyler can do the Rs through Zs. Think money and free advertising," Amanda told them sternly. "And be sure to keep track of your pledges so that Hero can enter them in the computer."

Amanda looked around for Tyler and found him staring at the lone computer as if it held some mysterious force.

"Come on, Tyler, let's do it," Amanda chastised him.

"At your service, madam," Tyler said, seating himself at Hero's desk and picking up the phone.

Rogue and Jamar noisily re-entered the main office area from the music mixing room, where they'd been lost in music talk.

"Say, where's my lady at?" Jamar asked, looking around for Keera.

"Oh, she split with Hero some time ago," Samantha offered before Amanda could reply.

"Really?" Rogue said archly, raising one eyebrow higher than the other.

"They went to put up the flyers to advertise the concert," Amanda said, glancing sharply at Samantha.

"Say what? Now she's busy handing out flyers. Yesterday, she—no, excuse me, her *mother*—tells me that Keera's too busy studying to come to the phone to talk to me. Studying, three weeks *before* school starts. Can you believe that?" Jamar said to Rogue as they walked over to Jamar's desk.

"Hey, man, I've always told you brainy chicks like Keera aren't going to wait around for players like us," Rogue told him. "Now that she's got her hold on you, she can get back to her real thing—studying—and you're always going to be second best."

"No way, Rogue," Jamar said. But he wasn't totally sure. "By the way, Amanda, did Keera say when she'd be back?" Jamar asked.

"They didn't say they were leaving, so I really couldn't say," Amanda replied with a slight edge to her voice. "I mean, I'm sure they'll be back soon. After all, they've been gone for over an hour."

"But who's counting?" Tyler asked jovially.

Just then, there was a clap of thunder outside, and a bolt of lightning lit up the sky. Rain fell in sheets, pummeling the ground below.

"Pretty tough to be out on a motorcycle hanging up posters in this storm," Tyler commented.

"Sure am glad it's not me," Rogue added.

Amanda gazed morosely at the drops spattering onto the window, half-expecting Hero and Keera to burst through the door any second.

This is stupid. I will not let this bother me, Amanda vowed, forcing herself to dial the next number on her list.

But Amanda couldn't help wondering what was going on.

Half an hour later, there was still no sign of Hero or Keera.

Amanda tried not to look at the clock every five minutes, but it was hopeless. Where could they be? she wondered.

"Sure is taking a long time to put up those posters," Rogue remarked cheerfully.

"Quit your jivin', man. It's beginning to get on my nerves," Jamar said.

"I'm sure Keera and Hero want to be very thorough," Amanda said through clenched teeth.

Samantha smiled a tiny smile to herself.

While Amanda and Jamar were pre-occupied with Hero's and Keera's absence, Tyler had managed to wend his way over to the financial computer, and he had worked there unnoticed for quite some time. Long enough to find out what he needed to know.

Now he stood in the doorway, arms stretched overhead. "Hey, you really run a sweatshop here, Amanda. How about we hit the Snack Shack and get something to eat?" Tyler suggested.

Amanda sighed heavily. Should she wait for Hero and Keera to come back, watching the second hand tick around the clock?

"I'm ready for something to eat," Rogue remarked, getting up from his chair.

Amanda looked over at Jamar. Jamar looked back at Amanda. Then they both looked quickly away.

"I could eat," Jamar said.

"Let's go, then," Amanda said defiantly.

Chapter Seven

Hero and Keera had no sooner handed out their last flyer and were on their way to the Snack Shack when Hero's motorcycle ground to a slow and unhappy-sounding halt.

"Uh-oh," Keera said. "I don't know anything about motorcycles, but this one sounds sick to me."

"Aw, man, I just went over this thing yesterday," Hero said in frustration, jumping off the bike and looking at the engine.

Keera peered down beneath the motorcycle, watching as Hero tried to figure out what had gone wrong. Long minutes passed as Hero tirelessly went over the entire motorcycle, sweat pouring down his face and sticking to his shirt.

Neither Hero nor Keera noticed the dark, swollen clouds that had taken over the sullen sky. The air grew silent and still.

After a while, Hero sat up. Grease streaked his forehead and spattered his arms and hands.

"Maybe we should call somebody to help us fix it," Keera suggested. "Like your dad or somebody."

"I don't have any way of getting in touch with my dad, and my mom's car is in the shop," Hero said grimly.

"My parents aren't around either," Keera remarked.

"And I don't exactly have the cash for a tow truck," Hero told her, resting his elbows on his knees for a moment. Feeling in his pockets, he pulled out a couple of fives, some nickels, three pennies, and some pocket lint. "In fact, I think it's safe to say the well is almost completely dry."

"Yeah, I don't even have a quarter for a phone. I forgot to take my pocketbook when I left home this morning." Keera was starting to feel a little nervous. "What are we going to do?"

Before Hero could reply, thunder shattered the air, and lightning flashed all around them.

Keera screamed. Hero leaped to his feet. Rain came down in great sheets of water, instantly drenching them both. Instinctively, Hero grabbed his saddlebag, pulled out his leather jacket, and protectively draped it over Keera's head, pulling her close to him. She was shaking like a leaf.

"We're only a few miles from the Snack Shack," Hero shouted over the downpour. "Maybe we'll meet someone we know there who can help us. Can you make it?"

Keera looked doubtful, but she nodded her head.

Together they began to sprint toward the restaurant. Rain splashed around them and ran down their faces.

At last Hero and Keera arrived at the Snack Shack, drenched and out of breath. Keera was panting and laughing uncontrollably. Thunderstorms always made her terrified and giddy. Her emotions were contagious. Hero couldn't help himself, and he started to laugh as well.

As they burst through the restaurant door, every head turned to look at them. Hero and Keera were so convulsed with laughter, they didn't notice Amanda, Tyler, Samantha, Rogue, and Jamar sitting at a large round table in the corner.

Amanda's face burned bright crimson with embarrassment. She knew exactly what Samantha and Tyler would be thinking. And, frankly, she wasn't sure just what to think herself.

Just then, Hero noticed Amanda and everyone else at the table. "Keera, look, the gang's all here," he said, leading Keera over to the table littered with empty plates and glasses. For a moment he forgot that his hair was plastered around his head and forehead and he was dripping wet.

Amanda eyed Hero's leather jacket, which Keera was still wearing over her shoulders. Water dripped from it, making small splashing sounds in the puddle forming at Keera's feet.

"Get all those flyers up?" Rogue commented calmly.

Mustering her dignity, Keera stuck out her chin and replied, "Yes, as a matter of fact, we did." She could feel the color rising hot in her cheeks.

"Keera, girl, you are soaking wet!" Jamar said with concern. He removed Hero's soaked leather jacket and replaced it with his purple and neon-green windbreaker.

"Didn't expect to see you two for the rest of the day," Tyler remarked.

Samantha tittered.

Hero looked over at Amanda. Her eyes met his for a moment, then glided away.

Seeing Hero and Keera laughing together had made Amanda's heart ache. She couldn't remember when she and Hero had ever laughed together like that.

"Hey, Amanda, what's up?" Hero asked. He wasn't sure what to make of Amanda's silence, but he knew that, with Samantha and Tyler around, it couldn't mean anything good.

"Nothing, just taking a break. While you've been out riding, Samantha, Tyler, and I have been trying to get advertising donations for the concert. You do remember the KSS-Off concert, don't you?"

Hero's eyes veiled over at Amanda's remark. But, before he could react, Keera spoke up.

"Oh, Amanda, you'll never believe what happened. Just as we put up the last flyer, Hero's motorcycle broke down. Hero spent over an hour trying to fix it, and then it started to pour, and we didn't have any money even for a phone call, so we ran the whole way here . . ." The words spilled feverishly out of Keera's mouth.

But after Amanda's cutting remark, Hero wasn't interested in explaining anything to anyone. Turning swiftly on his heel, Hero walked over to the far side of the restaurant, flung himself into a booth, and buried his face in the menu.

Immediately Amanda was contrite. "I'll drive Hero back in my car and meet you guys at the station," Amanda said quickly.

Amanda jumped up, her chair scraping against the checkerboard tile floor, and went over to Hero's booth, slipping into the seat beside him. "I'm sorry," she said softly.

Hero didn't look up from the menu.

"It's just that I didn't know what to think with you and Keera gone so long, without even a good-bye, and I saw her kiss you when she got on your motorcycle, and then . . . " Amanda's voice trailed off. She couldn't remember why she'd gotten so upset.

"You were jealous of me going off with Keera?" Hero asked, incredulous at the thought.

Amanda blushed and cast her eyes downward. "Pretty stupid, huh?" she replied.

"Incredibly," Hero said with a grin. "But, you know, I kind of like the idea that you're jealous."

"Well, don't get too attached to the idea," Amanda said. "I don't intend to do it again!"

"You know there's no one else in the world for me but you, Amanda," Hero said softly.

Then, ever so gently, Hero took Amanda's face in his hands and gazed directly into her luminous violet eyes. Amanda placed her hand behind Hero's head, stroking the soft, silky hair that curled damply at the nape of his neck, slowly bringing his lips to hers.

In that moment, the rest of the world fell away.

Chapter Eight

The next day, Amanda pulled her white Mustang convertible up in front of Hero's house and tooted the horn. Hero had told her not to bother ringing the doorbell, since he'd be out back in the garage, working on his motorcycle.

Amanda felt funny not going in to say hello to Hero's parents, whom she had never met. Catching a glimpse of Mrs. Montoya standing at the window, Amanda waved. Mrs. Montoya smiled warmly and waved back.

At the sound of Amanda's horn, Hero sauntered out from behind the house and stepped into Amanda's car.

After a quick kiss, Amanda put the car into gear, and they rode off.

Hair blowing in the wind, Amanda glanced over at Hero. As always, her heart skipped a beat when she caught him unawares. His face was so perfect, his expression so intense. But half the time it seemed as though he were somewhere else, thinking about something . . . or maybe *someone* else, Amanda thought. She quickly pushed that thought right out of her mind.

Impulsively, Amanda reached out and stroked Hero's jaw with one finger. "Why so serious?" she asked.

"Oh, it's just that I finally figured out what happened to my motorcycle. Somehow, water got into the oil tank, and it really screwed up the engine. I'm going to have to take the whole thing apart and grease it before she'll be ready to ride."

"How could something like that happen?" Amanda asked.

Hero didn't say what he was thinking: somebody had sabotaged his bike. He was keeping his suspicions to himself.

"Well, you can fix anything," Amanda said confidently. "Look what a brilliant job you did with the computer ticketing system. With the phone ringing off the hook as we were leaving the station yesterday afternoon, it looked like it was doing the job. I'll bet at ten dollars a

ticket—and with the advertising donations we've been promised —we've
already taken in a good chunk of the
$10,000 we need to fund KSS for the rest
of the summer and cover the concert
expenses."

"It's all because of those flyers Keera
and I put up," Hero said, teasing Amanda.

"Or maybe those hundred-and-one
phone calls I made yesterday asking for
advertising," Amanda responded,
punching him lightly on his hard
shoulder.

Amanda pulled her car up to the curb
in front of the station. "Ride's over,"
Amanda said. But she stayed seated as
Hero got out of the car.

"Aren't you coming in?" Hero asked,
surprised.

"I'll be back in a while. Keera and I got
to talking last night, and we thought it
might be a good plan to do on-the-spot
interviews with kids in Cliffside, asking
them how important Student KSS-TV is to
them," Amanda replied. "We could run
the interviews between music sets."

"Cool idea," Hero said.

"Thanks," Amanda said. "So, I'm supposed to be meeting her at the corner of Main and Cliffside in . . . oh, no, about two minutes!" Amanda added, checking her watch.

Reluctant to let her leave, Hero leaned through the car window, seeking Amanda's mouth with his own. He kissed Amanda softly, tenderly, fingering her silky blonde hair, gently caressing her soft, smooth cheek.

For a moment, Amanda forgot she was sitting in her car in the middle of a street. When Hero pulled away, it left Amanda breathless, her heart pounding in her chest and her face flushed with heat.

"Later," Hero said.

"Later," Amanda called, sighing as she watched Hero's strong, muscular form moving away from her.

When Hero walked into the KSS station, he was surprised to find Samantha sitting at Amanda's desk.

"Hey," Hero said shortly. Then looking around, he asked, "Where is everyone?"

"Drew had to go out, Jamar's working on something back in the music studio, and Tyler's around somewhere. I don't know where Amanda and Keera are. Drew asked me to hold down the fort and answer the phones that aren't hooked up to the computer. I keep hoping Nick Ganos or Jamie West will call. After all, we could end up being very good friends, and I'm sure . . . "

Hero only half-listened as Samantha chattered on. After looking through the notes on his desk, Hero decided to check the ticket-order printout.

As Hero was about to get up from his desk, he looked up to find Samantha standing above him. Quickly perching on the corner of his desk, Samantha crossed her tanned legs and smiled coyly at Hero.

"What's up, Samantha?" Hero asked.

"Oh, I was just thinking how exciting this is, you and me here alone together, getting ready for the hottest concert to ever hit Cliffside," Samantha said, practically slithering along the desk.

For a moment, Hero's face held no expression. Then a small smile played around his lips.

"What are you thinking about, Hero?" Samantha asked in a husky whisper, leaning closer still.

Hero stood, brought his face down to Samantha's, crooked his finger under her chin, and gently tilted her face up toward his.

"Do you really want to know?" Hero asked, bringing his face toward Samantha's.

Barely able to contain herself, Samantha whispered, "Oh, yes."

"Computer printouts," Hero said calmly, gazing solemnly into Samantha's eyes. Then he winked and headed for the computer room.

Samantha stared after Hero, incredulous.

"I guess if you're going to two-time Amanda, Keera's more your type, then, is that it?" Samantha remarked nastily to Hero's departing back.

Hero whirled around and glared icily at Samantha. But, before he could reply, Tyler sauntered into the main room. Noting the tension, Tyler pointedly maneuvered past Hero and positioned himself alongside Samantha.

"Hey, Samantha, what's doing?" Tyler asked, never taking his eyes from Hero.

"Oh, just checking up on some stuff for Amanda with Hero, here," Samantha said, her eyes darting wickedly from Hero to Tyler.

Hero pressed his lips together, the skin

around his mouth tightening to white. For Amanda's sake, he wasn't going to get into it with these two, but it was taking all the self-control he had.

"Hope you got the point, then, Samantha," Hero said meaningfully.

"Oh, I did, Hero, thanks," Samantha answered sweetly.

"Good," Hero said with a short nod. Then he turned and went back to the computer room.

"What was that all about?" Tyler asked, casually walking over to Hero's desk and rifling through the computer notes there.

"Nothing much," Samantha answered. She wasn't about to tell Tyler that Hero wasn't interested in her, either.

Chapter Nine

*S*everal hours later, Amanda and Keera burst into the station. Amanda was happy and relaxed, chattering a mile a minute about the interviews they'd just finished. Keera, on the other hand, was looking a little stressed. She'd been up late doing practice SAT tests the night before, and her scores had been less than stellar.

"Where is everybody?" Amanda asked, poking her head into Drew's office.

Drew looked up from his desk. "Samantha and Tyler went to lunch. Hero and Jamar are in the back." Drew found the papers he'd been searching for and, with a short wave, headed for the door. "Got an important lunch date. See you later," he called back over his shoulder.

Just then, Hero came into the main office. He broke into a delighted grin at the sight of Amanda.

"Hey! How are the roving reporters?" Hero asked Amanda and Keera.

"Great! We got some terrific interviews. Everyone we talked to wanted the show to stay on the air—and not just kids, either. Adults like and watch us, too!"

"How are the ticket sales coming?" Keera asked. She could hear the computer busily printing away in the other room.

"We're doing pretty well," Hero said proudly. "I'll have a progress report for Drew for the weekly meeting. We can total up the ticket sales and other donations then."

"Say, does anybody know where my man the music Jam is?" Rogue said. Keera whirled, started. She hadn't noticed him standing against the doorway.

"You mean *my* man, don't you?" Keera remarked sharply.

Rogue looked at Keera thoughtfully for a moment, his shiny black eyes glittering under the fluorescent lights.

"Uh, Amanda, how about we grab something to eat—maybe at the Snack Shack?" Hero suggested, hoping to break the tension.

Amanda looked over at Keera and Rogue.

"Do either of you guys want to come to lunch?" Amanda asked. She got no reply.

"Okay, then—I guess we'll see you folks later," Amanda said brightly to the air. Then she grabbed Hero by the elbow, and the two made a quick exit.

"Listen up, Keera. Why don't you stick to your books and let Jamar alone—" Rogue started to say.

"No, *you* listen up, Rogue," Keera snapped, all the tension of the past week bursting forth. "You have been in my face for an entire month. *I'm* the one who's going out with Jamar, not you. I don't try to get between the two of you, and I want you to butt out of *my* life—period!"

Just then, Jamar entered the office, grinning happily.

"Hey, dude. Wait till you hear what I've been working on. Keera, after Rogue and I get done in the music room, you'll help me finish those food-stand calls, right?" Jamar asked.

Keera didn't say a word.

"Hey, what's happening, girlfriend?" Jamar went on blithely.

"What's happening? What's happening? I'll tell you what's *not* happening.

You and me making food-stand calls, that's what's not happening. Make your own calls. Or, better yet, get your Rogue-dude to help you make them. I'm out of here—I've got things to do." Keera turned on her heel and stalked out of the station.

"What was that all about?" Jamar asked Rogue.

"I've told you a hundred times, man, the chick's high-strung. She's got pressure on the brain. Keera's just not your type, man—you're better off without her," Rogue said.

Jamar paused for a moment. Maybe Rogue was right. Then he thought about not seeing Keera, not being able to kiss her soft, full mouth, or run his fingers lightly over the smooth, mocha skin of her arms. Not having Keera to talk to—about his family, about his music. And he thought about the special song he'd been working on.

"You don't know what you're talking about, dude," Jamar told Rogue, rousing himself into action. He raced out of the station, leaped onto his bicycle, and began pedaling after Keera's station wagon.

At the first red traffic light, Jamar pulled

up alongside Keera's open window. "Keera!" he yelled. "We have to talk."

"There's nothing to talk about," Keera said, refusing to meet Jamar's glance. The light changed, and she drove away.

Jamar pedaled so fast and furiously after her that he looked like a neon-green blur.

At the second red traffic light, Jamar, huffing and puffing, pulled up again. "Keera, please, just give me a minute," Jamar pleaded with her.

Keera rested her forehead on the steering wheel, not sure what to do. The light turned green and the car behind Keera's honked impatiently.

"Take it slow, man!" Jamar called behind him. Then he turned back to Keera. "Please?" Jamar asked again quietly, putting his hand inside the car window and touching Keera's arm.

At the pressure of his touch, Keera shivered. Goose bumps formed up and down her arm. Without a word, Keera pulled the car over to the curb.

Jamar slid into the worn front seat next to her and gently took her by the shoulders, searching her face with his eyes. "What's going on with you, Keera? Tell me," he asked.

Keera drew in a long, shaky breath. "I just think that, with everything going on at KSS, and with the studying my parents want me to do before school starts, it might be a good idea if we . . . if we . . ." Keera stopped, her throat closing as she choked back her tears.

"If we what?" Jamar asked, dreading her answer. "Come on, Keera. You don't have to spend your life doing what your parents want you to do. Lighten up, let go a little. Life's supposed to be fun, not all work, work, work, like your parents think. Who cares about those stupid SATs, anyway? It's just some scam those educational testers came up with to get people's money."

"You think life is some kind of game?" Keera asked. "Just play music all day and party with your friends? Well, I'm not like that. I've got to be serious and think about my responsibilities. Besides, you're too busy jamming with your band or letting Rogue tell you what to do to have any time left for me."

"Aw, Keera, I know we haven't spent

much time together lately, but I'll make it up to you after the concert, I promise," Jamar apologized. "I've been working on this really big surprise for the concert, and—"

"Jamar, I can't talk about this anymore. Not now. I have to go. Maybe we can talk some other time, after I've had a chance to think everything through," Keera said stiffly. She looked away from Jamar so he wouldn't see the tears poised in her eyes.

Keera saw Jamar's face crumple. For a moment, Keera regretted what she'd said. She wished that Jamar would cover her mouth with his full and tender lips, taking over her senses as her body melted into his.

Instead, Jamar simply slipped out of the car, shut the door, and slowly went over to his bicycle.

Keera pulled herself together and started up the car. She watched Jamar stand on the street, his arms dangling, empty, by his sides.

How did this all get so wrong? they each wondered.

At the Snack Shack, Hero and Amanda were finishing up their usual Shack lunch—double chiliburgers with atomic fries and triple chocolate milkshakes. It never failed to amaze Hero that Amanda could eat every bit as much as he did, and enjoy it. Other girls he'd known were always on endless diets, or else they acted like a burger and fries was the closest thing a restaurant had to a nuclear weapon.

Hero liked to watch Amanda. He loved the way the light sparkled from somewhere inside her lavender eyes, the high color that always tinted her softly tanned cheeks, and the way a small smile always hovered around the corners of her mouth, as if she was thinking of something funny all the time.

"I'm glad we got out of the station before the fireworks between Rogue and Keera started," Amanda said, popping the last atomic fry into her mouth. "But I'm surprised that Tyler and Samantha didn't end up here for lunch, too," Amanda added, peering around the room one last time. "I could have sworn that was Tyler's dad's Beamer in the parking lot."

"I had a good time without anyone else around," Hero said pointedly, not mentioning any names.

Amanda placed her hand on top of Hero's as he fiddled with a sugar packet.

"Oh, Hero, Tyler and Samantha aren't really so bad," Amanda said quietly. "Samantha's been my best friend for as long as I can remember."

Hero's face darkened at Amanda's remark. Some friend, he thought to himself.

Pulling her hand away, Amanda said, "You know, Hero, it would be a lot easier for me if you'd at least make an effort to like my friends."

Hero sat in silence. He was torn between telling Amanda how Samantha had pulled a move on him and protecting her from Samantha's treachery.

"After all, if you had some friends you really cared about, I would try to get along with them," Amanda said.

"With friends like Samantha, I'd get a sore neck from watching my back," Hero commented.

"What's that supposed to mean?" Amanda asked shortly.

"Forget it," Hero said. "It doesn't mean anything."

"No, I won't forget it. What are you

101

trying to say?" Amanda asked, her voice rising.

"Listen, Amanda. This isn't something to make a big scene about, and I don't want to hurt your feelings or anything, but I just don't think Samantha is much of a friend."

"Really? And why is that?" Amanda challenged, her eyes flashing.

"Well, if you want to know, Samantha came on to me when we were alone in the office this morning."

"Oh, she's just a flirt. You probably took it the wrong way," Amanda said dismissively.

"Amanda, I know the difference between flirting and interest. And I'm telling you, if I'd even met her a quarter of the way, I'd be busy doing something other than having lunch with you right now," Hero assured her.

For a moment, Amanda was too angry to speak.

"I can't believe you would do something like this," she sputtered at last.

"Me? What have I done?" Hero asked, incredulous at Amanda's anger.

"You are so desperate to make me

jealous again, just to satisfy your own pitiable ego, that you're willing to sabotage my friendship with Samantha! Well, I'm not buying into it. Oh, Hero, how could you?" Amanda said, ready to burst into tears.

Without another word, Hero got up, threw down some bills to cover the check, and stormed out of the restaurant.

Dramatic exit number thirty, Amanda thought to herself, getting up from the table. Only this time, she wasn't going after him. This time, he'd just gone too far.

Chapter Ten

*W*hen Amanda and Hero entered the Snack Shack, Tyler and Samantha sunk down low in their booth so as not to be seen.

They were delighted when Amanda and Hero chose the booth next to theirs. Not wanting to be discovered, Tyler and Samantha hadn't been able to let out a single breath. As their reward, they had been able to overhear every word of Amanda's conversation with Hero.

"So, you're putting the moves on old Hero, eh?" Tyler said in a low, leering voice when he was sure that Amanda had moved out of hearing distance.

Samantha blushed. "Maybe. Why— would it bother you if I did?" Samantha asked, hoping to get a rise out of Tyler.

"Why would it bother me if *you* went out with Hero? It bothers me that

Amanda is going out with Hero," Tyler said carelessly.

Then he thought for a moment. "But it's not a bad idea," he added, a wicked light gleaming from his steely blue eyes.

"What do you mean by that?" Samantha's curiosity was piqued, even though she was burning inside at Tyler's rebuff.

"I mean, maybe there's a way to eliminate Hero from Amanda's life entirely," Tyler said.

"Well, they certainly don't sound like they're living happily ever after right now," Samantha said, indicating the door Hero had just slammed.

"Yeah, but that's the way they are. They fight, they make up, they fight, they make up, they . . . kiss." Tyler made a wry face as if repulsed by the thought. "At the end of the day, Hero will still be in my face," Tyler added.

"So, what's your point, Tyler?" Samantha asked.

"I've got a plan in the works for Hero, but, for Amanda's sake, I intend to look like Mr. Perfect so I can get past that whole motorcycle race fiasco. I can't say anything against Hero. But *you* can get between Amanda and Hero before they make up again," Tyler said, pursing his lips into a long, tight smile. "Then you'll get what you want—which is Hero, right? And I'll get what I want—Amanda."

"Well, I don't know," Samantha said hesitantly.

"Oh, come on, Samantha. This way everybody's happy," Tyler said firmly.

Then he explained his idea to Samantha, who listened very carefully to everything Tyler said.

After lunch, Amanda headed over to the KSS station. She wondered how Hero was going to make it back, or if he was even going to come back to the station today.

How could Hero be so vile? Amanda thought, as she set up her interview tape to run on the visual mixer monitor in the control room. Wanting me to be jealous of him and Samantha. That's even more ridiculous than Hero and Keera, Amanda thought, replaying the scene with Hero at the Snack Shack.

Amanda forced her mind back into the

control room. That's it. No more thinking about Hero, Amanda thought to herself firmly. I'm going to edit these on-the-town interviews, and I'm not going to let Hero and his crazy need for me to be jealous get in the way.

Amanda was just about to wrap up her editing session for the day, when Samantha knocked at the control room door.

"Amanda, I need a break from the phone. Mind if I come in?" Samantha asked.

Stretching back in her chair, Amanda replied, "I wish you would. I'm almost done here for today, anyway."

"You know, Amanda, I'm glad to help you guys out, but my tongue hurts from asking so many people for donations," Samantha admitted, plopping down in a chair.

Amanda laughed. She remembered that was what she liked best about Samantha: she always said what was on her mind.

Looking at her friend, Amanda felt a rush of affection. A kaleidoscope of memories flashed through her mind. She remembered the time when they were seven years old. She and Samantha had gotten into a fight with Tyler and decided to start a No-Boys-Allowed Club in the backyard of Amanda's old house.

In retaliation, Tyler had started a No-Girls-Allowed Club of his own. But, of course, since Amanda and Samantha were his only friends at the time, he sat there alone in his clubhouse for what must have seemed like forever, before deciding to dress up like GI Joe and storm their clubhouse doors. After a long and heated battle, they all made up and forgot about the clubs.

Or the time when they were ten years old, and they crept into Tyler's cabin at Camp Winnitaki and poured honey on all the sleeping boys' hands. Amanda smiled mischievously as she remembered Tyler telling them how the boys woke up with the raccoons and the camp dog and cat all licking their hands in the middle of the night. Samantha and Amanda had laughed and laughed.

Amanda smiled at Samantha. "You know, it means a lot to me that you and Tyler are helping out with the concert and trying to keep KSS going," she said.

"No big deal," Samantha said uncomfortably.

"What's wrong?" Amanda asked.

"Oh, just . . . nothing," Samantha said, shaking her head.

"Come on, Samantha—something's bothering you. What is it?" Amanda asked with concern.

Samantha lowered her eyes for a moment and flushed. Then, biting her lower lip, she said, "Well, I have to tell you something. It's kind of upsetting, and I'm not sure whether or not I should say it."

"You can tell me anything, Samantha. You're my best friend," Amanda reassured her.

"Well, this morning, when I was here by myself on the phone . . ." Samantha broke off.

"Yes," Amanda encouraged her.

"Well, I was minding my own business, and, all of a sudden, Hero came up behind me and put his hands on my shoulders, saying I looked like I could use a good massage." Samantha glanced quickly at Amanda's face. Seeing the shock there, she continued rapidly, "I was so surprised

I could barely move. Before I knew what was happening, he started rubbing my shoulders and my neck, and nuzzling his face into my hair. I pulled away and told him that you were my best friend, and I wasn't about to let him ruin that. And he told me that there wasn't any reason you had to know about it."

Amanda felt like she'd been punched in the stomach. Hero going after Samantha? Amanda couldn't believe it. Then Amanda's eyes narrowed. So that was why Hero came up with that ridiculous story about Samantha coming on to him. He wanted to make sure he told his story first before she heard the truth from Samantha. Suddenly her mother's words echoed in her mind: "You don't really know anything about this boy at all."

Amanda looked over at Samantha, who was teary-eyed and biting her lip.

"You know, Samantha, I wasn't even going to tell you this, but now I feel like I have to. Hero told me at lunch that *you* propositioned him this morning, and that *he* was the one who turned you down," Amanda said.

Samantha caught her breath. "How

could he try to break up our friendship like this?" she wailed.

"Well, he's not going to, that's all there is to it," Amanda assured her.

"You mean, you're not going to go out with him anymore?" Samantha asked, turning her tear-filled eyes to look into Amanda's.

Amanda thought for a moment. Could she really forget about Hero, even after this last betrayal? Looking at Samantha's red and teary face, Amanda decided, she could. She hadn't felt this close to Samantha in a very long time.

"Don't worry, Samantha, I won't let Hero or any guy ever come between us."

Remembering an oath they'd taken when they were twelve never to let a boy come between them, Samantha said, smiling through her tears, "Do you swear?"

"I swear," Amanda said, hugging Samantha. "It's really over between Hero and me."

Chapter Eleven

*T*he next day at the weekly progress meeting, Drew asked everyone for updates on their projects. Amanda spoke up first.

"Keera and I finished our on-the-town interviews, and I'm almost done with the final edit. I was hoping you could go through it with me?" Amanda said, looking questioningly at Drew.

"Love to," Drew said, giving her his quick and easy grin.

"As far as donations go, we've got all the equipment and stagehand help we'll need to set up for the concert," Amanda said proudly.

"Way to go, Amanda," Jamar and Rogue cheered. Everyone else clapped politely.

"How about money contributions?" Drew asked.

"Local businesses called so far are committed to donating $2,900—thanks mostly to the hours of calls that Tyler and Samantha have made," Amanda said.

"And we won't stop until we get to Z or lose our voices trying, whichever comes first," Tyler said gallantly. Amanda flashed him a quick, grateful smile.

Hero rolled his eyes at Tyler's remark. Amanda glimpsed Hero's reaction from the corner of her eye, and her smile froze on her lips.

Neither Hero nor Amanda had spoken to the other since yesterday. After what Samantha had told her, Amanda wasn't planning to ever speak to Hero again.

"What's doing with publicity?" Drew asked Keera.

"All the local radio and television stations have gotten their press releases, and they've promised to talk up the concert every chance they get," she reported.

Jamar nodded in agreement. "I've heard them advertising the concert whenever I've tuned in."

He looked over to Keera to see her reaction, but Jamar could have been talking in a foreign language for all the attention Keera was paying him.

"That leaves concessions and music," Drew said.

"Jamar and Rogue have been handling that on their own," she said pointedly.

Exchanging a gleeful look with Rogue, Jamar said, "Joe's Burgers and Dogs, Chicken King, and the Snack Shack all said they would set up food stands, and . . ." Jamar paused dramatically, "Rogue and I convinced them to give us twenty-five percent of what they take in!"

Everyone shouted their approval. Even Keera mustered a small smile.

"As for the music, Nick Ganos says he'll play two sets, and Jamie West committed the Jezebels to two sets. But the best part is, Grim Reaper is going to play one set with . . . JellyJam!" Jamar announced with a proud flourish.

"Great job." Drew grinned at them all. "It sounds like almost everything is under control. And now the final order of business," Drew said. He turned toward Hero, who was leaning against the far wall of the room, apart from the rest of the group.

"Ticket sales are great. As of yesterday,

we've sold 324 tickets, and $3,240 is already deposited into the ticket account at the bank. And we still have two days left to the concert. We can also sell tickets at the door, but I don't think we'll really need to count on those," Hero said matter-of-factly.

Drew beamed. "You did a smooth job setting up that ticket program, Hero. It's going great."

"Our Hero," Samantha sighed mockingly.

Hero gave Samantha a cool smile. Then he glanced over at Amanda. Amanda's face colored hotly, and she refused to meet Hero's glance.

No one noticed Tyler's eyes glowing maliciously at Drew's remark.

"Okay," Drew said, scribbling as he spoke. "So far, we can count on $2,900 from business donations, $3,240 from ticket sales . . ." Drew calculated rapidly. "That's $6,140 so far. We need at least $10,000 to keep things going until September and to cover the cost of the concert, so that leaves us with two more days to make about $3,800. With the money from the food sales, plus whatever tickets we sell in the next two days . . . well, I guess we might make it," Drew said.

There was a solemn silence.

"Maybe we should all start calling to solicit donations," Amanda suggested.

"That might help." Drew said.

"Who's left to call?" Keera asked.

"Well, yesterday, I left off at the beginning of the M's in the Yellow Pages, and Tyler, you got all the way up to the T's, didn't you?" Samantha asked.

"I think so," Tyler answered.

"So, if we each take two letters of the alphabet, we could be done calling by lunchtime," Amanda said enthusiastically.

"Let's get to it, then," Jamar said. Immediately the group broke up and headed for the phones scattered around the office.

Tyler and Hero arrived at Hero's desk at the same time. Hero emphatically sat down and swung around in his chair, claiming it for his own.

"Tyler, you can use the fax phone in Drew's computer room," Amanda offered.

"Sure, Tyler, go ahead," Drew agreed. "I'm going out for a while anyway."

"Thanks," Tyler said, keeping his feeling of triumph to himself.

He had some work to do on Hero's computer.

Several hours and many phone calls later, everyone regrouped for another update.

"So, folks, it looks as though we've gotten another . . . $2,230, if I've added all your figures correctly," Drew said, knitting his eyebrows in concentration as he punched everyone's totals into his pocket calculator.

"Ticket sales for today?" Drew asked Hero.

"I haven't had a chance to calculate today's sales yet," Hero said, "but I can do that after our meeting and go over it with you later."

Drew nodded.

"Well, we're still over $1,600 short—but if we sell another 100 tickets between today and the concert, and we plan on twenty-five percent of the food receipts, which will probably be something like five dollars a person . . . " Drew rapidly punched the figures into the calculator. "I think we'll make it. But everything will depend on those ticket sales—so, Hero, let's get to that update as soon as we can," Drew said brusquely.

"Will do," Hero said.

"I'm going out to get something to eat. Does anybody want me to bring them back anything?" Tyler asked. "Want to come, Amanda?"

"No, thanks anyway, Tyler. Kit came home last night from sleepaway camp, and the brat-sister made me promise, in front of my parents, to take her clothes-shopping at the mall—so now I really have to do it," Amanda said with fake dismay.

"Well, see you later then," Tyler said, running out the door. No one saw him wink slyly to Samantha and point to the back door of the station.

"What's his hurry?" Amanda asked Samantha.

"You know Tyler," Samantha said lightly, not wanting to dwell on Tyler's quick exit. She knew he was planning to be back just as soon as everyone was out of the way so he could play around with Hero's computer.

"I guess," Amanda said. "Hey, Keera, Samantha, do you want to come with us to the mall?"

"Thanks, Amanda, but I've got to get home and do some more studying," Keera said, looking anxious to leave as well. "My mother's really been after me this past week."

"Keera, I'd really like to talk to you," Jamar interrupted then.

"I-I-I can't right now, Jamar. I don't have anything to say," Keera said in a low voice.

"Hey, Jammin' man, let's go over to my place so we can fine-tune the finale," Rogue said loudly.

Keera threw Rogue a disdainful look, then quickly collected her things.

Jamar stood still, torn between following his heart or his friend. Just then, Jamar's phone rang. Automatically, Rogue picked it up. His eyes went round behind his shades as he listened to the voice on the other end of the phone.

"Jammer, it's for you," Rogue said, handing him the phone.

Keera's face closed as Jamar took the phone in his hand. Ignoring the pleading glance he threw in her direction, Keera spun on her heel and left the station.

"What about you, Samantha?" Amanda asked.

"I think I'm going to go back over my list and try to connect with some of the business people I missed," Samantha said, looking over her notes. "I mean, every penny counts, right? Besides, I keep hoping I'll be the one to pick up the phone if Nick Ganos and Jamie West call in."

"Okay, I'll talk to you later," Amanda said. Amanda glanced briefly in the direction of the computer room. Then she looked over at Samantha, who seemed totally involved in dialing the phone.

With a quick shake of her head, Amanda dismissed any suspicious thoughts about Samantha and Hero. After all, Drew was there. Besides, Hero had already made his play, and Samantha had told him to get lost. What more could possibly happen?

Chapter Twelve

 B y the time Jamar got off the phone and raced outside, Keera was long gone. Determined to catch up with her, Jamar hopped on his bicycle and started pedaling furiously.

When Jamar got to Keera's house, he was surprised to see that the old battered station wagon wasn't parked out front. Nevertheless, he went up to the door and rang the bell, hoping that Keera would answer instead of her mother.

Akim, Keera's seven-year-old brother, peered out the window. Seeing Jamar at the door, his face split into a big grin.

"I got it, Mom. It's for me," Akim called, flinging the door open wide.

"Hey, Jammin' dude, come on in and play with me," Akim greeted Jamar enthusiastically.

"Hey, little dude, where's your

beautiful sister?" Jamar said.

"Aw, Keera's at the library again, studying," Akim said, wrinkling his nose. "She says I make too much noise."

"Well, how about we make some noise together, then?" Jamar suggested. "At least until your sister gets home!"

"Cool!" Akim shouted with glee. "Come on, let's play ball!"

Keera stiffened when she saw Jamar's bicycle parked in front of her house. Hearing Akim's happy shouts, Keera could tell they were out back shooting hoops.

Wearily, Keera dropped her books in the front hall and went to the kitchen at the back of the house. Peeking out the window, unnoticed, Keera watched as Jamar and Akim played a mean game of one-on-one. By some miracle, Akim managed to score shot after shot, while a mock-angry Jamar never seemed to make a single basket. Keera smiled to herself.

For a moment, watching the sheer pleasure on the faces of Akim and Jamar, she forgot all about studying, and work, and her mother's opinion of "no-good, shiftless musicians."

Jamar really was like a little kid sometimes. Catching him unawares, Keera remembered what she loved about Jamar: the way his eyes crinkled when he laughed, the way his lips felt, soft and full against her own.

Against her will, Keera found herself smiling. Just then, Jamar happened to look up and catch Keera's smile. Surprised and happy, Jamar gave her a dazzling, happy smile in return.

"Keera, honey, is that you? How did your practice SAT go today?" her mother called from upstairs.

Remembering her less than perfect score, Keera's face pinched tensely into a mask of worry.

"It went okay, Ma," Keera told her as Mrs. Johnson entered the kitchen.

"Just okay, Keera? That doesn't sound very encouraging," Mrs. Johnson said. For the first time, she noticed that Jamar was out back with Akim.

"Did you spend your day with that Jammin' boy again, instead of doing your studying?" Mrs. Johnson asked sternly.

"No, Ma, of course not," Keera replied. "He was here when I got here."

"I thought you told me you weren't seeing him anymore," Mrs. Johnson said.

"Well . . ." Keera's voice caught in her throat.

"Then what's he doing here?"

"I don't know," Keera said faintly, as Jamar entered the kitchen through the back door with Akim in close pursuit.

"Hey, Mrs. Johnson. You're looking lovely today," Jamar said respectfully, giving her his most charming smile.

"Hmmmm, save that kind of stuff for your songwriting," Mrs. Johnson said.

"Okay," Jamar said agreeably. Then he turned the full force of his smile on Keera. "Hey, Keera," Jamar said softly, his eyes pleading with her to welcome him.

"Hey," Keera replied in a noncommittal voice.

"Can we talk?" Jamar asked quietly.

"Dinner will be ready in ten minutes. Akim, you take yourself right upstairs and get washed. Keera, you get ready for dinner, too," Mrs. Johnson said.

Jamar followed Keera into the front room. Keera didn't know which way to turn. She knew that if she looked directly into Jamar's eyes, she could never say what had to be said.

"Keera," Jamar began, excitement sparkling in his eyes. "I have something really important to tell you."

Jamar had written a song dedicated especially to Keera. And that phone call he'd received at the station just as Keera had walked out the door had been from Nick Ganos. He'd agreed to have his band, Grim Reaper, play Keera's song *with* the JellyJam band at the KSS-Off concert.

It was the single most exciting thing that had ever happened to Jamar, and the only person he felt like sharing it with was Keera.

"I have something important to tell you, too," Keera said, choking on the words.

"You, first," Jamar said generously, too caught up in his own excitement to notice Keera's distress.

"Well, I've been thinking a lot about you, and about me. I mean, about us," Keera began, not able to look in Jamar's eyes.

Jamar's enthusiasm faded away. His eyes grew round, and he stood very still, staring at Keera.

"Keera, honey, dinner's almost ready,"

Mrs. Johnson interrupted insistently from the kitchen.

"Maybe right now isn't such a good time to talk," Jamar suggested hopefully.

"No, I mean, yes. It is. A good time, I mean. Because I've got a lot of studying to do, and . . . and . . . I-I-I-I don't think we sh-sh-sh-should—" Keera stuttered as she tried to get out the words.

Swiftly, Jamar crossed the length of the room and took Keera in his arms, pressing her closely to him. It was too much for Keera to bear. She began sobbing softly against Jamar's shirt.

"Sssssh, pretty Keera, ssssh. It's going to be all right. You've been studying too hard, girl. You've got to lighten up, try to have a little fun," Jamar said soothingly.

"No, no, that's not what this is about," Keera protested, her voice muffled against Jamar's chest.

"Sure it is," he said, gently stroking her soft, curling hair. "I have an idea. How about we go out to dinner, just the two of us, right now?" Jamar asked eagerly.

"Keeeeeera," Mrs. Johnson called impatiently.

"No, I can't. I've got to go," Keera said,

tearing herself away from the comfort of Jamar's arms. "And you'd better go, too," Keera said, leading him to the front door.

"I'll call you later then," Jamar said insistently, half in and half out of the doorway.

"Good-bye, Jamar," Keera said, feeling miserable and confused.

"Bye, Keera," Jamar said, stepping backward onto the porch.

Without another word, Keera shut the door. She stared at its wooden panels, knowing that Jamar was doing exactly the same thing on the other side of the door.

Chapter Thirteen

Amanda had just left the KSS station when Hero sauntered into the office. He stopped when he saw Samantha was the only one there.

"Is Amanda gone?" Hero asked.

"Like the wind," Samantha told him, giving him a radiant smile.

"Oh," Hero said, disappointed. He'd been hoping to speak with her before she left. "Have you seen Drew?"

"He was here just a minute ago," Samantha said, looking around. "I'm sure he'll be back any moment. Is there something I can do for you?" she added coquettishly, strolling over to Hero.

"Nothing I can think of," Hero said firmly, beating a hasty retreat back into the computer room.

Samantha was so intent on ensnaring Hero in conversation, she tripped over a bump in the rug and landed in a crumpled and most ungraceful heap.

Immediately, Hero was at her side. "Are you okay?" he asked, kneeling beside her.

Samantha realized this could be the opportunity she needed to get Hero out of the station and give Tyler the time he needed to sneak back into the station to get at the computer.

Samantha's face crinkled in pain. "I think I really hurt my ankle," she told Hero, wincing as she tried to flex her right foot.

"Maybe I should get you some ice," Hero offered.

But Samantha put her hand gently on Hero's arm, keeping him beside her. "No, don't leave yet. I mean, let's give it a few minutes and then I'll see how I feel. Would you mind helping me over to the chair?" Samantha asked, tilting her head prettily as she gazed deeply into Hero's endlessly dark eyes.

Hero slipped his arm around Samantha's waist and helped her limp over to Amanda's desk chair.

Just then, Drew re-entered the office. What's wrong?" he asked.

"Oh, clumsy me, I fell and hurt my ankle," Samantha said.

"Are you okay? Should I get you to a doctor?" Drew asked with concern.

"No, no, I'll be fine in a few minutes," Samantha assured him.

"Well, okay, if you're sure." Turning to Hero, Drew asked, "Have you got the latest ticket sales figures printed out yet?"

"I do, and things are looking pretty good. There are just one or two things I wanted to talk about—"

Samantha groaned, interrupting Hero.

"Maybe that ankle is more serious than you think," Drew said. "Someone should help you get home so you can put that leg up and get some ice on it." Looking at his watch, he added, "I've got to go to a meeting with some very big money people to talk about funding for the year. Hero, do you think you'd be able to give Samantha a ride home?"

Feeling trapped, Hero replied, "Well, sure, no problem. But, Drew, I thought we were going to go over the ticket sales—"

"I'll come back to review it later, after my meeting. Leave it on my desk, and we'll go over it together in the morning,"

Drew interrupted him. "Hero, remember to lock up. Later, folks!" Drew said, rushing out the door.

"Guess that leaves you and me," Samantha said, a wicked gleam in her eye.

"Right. We can split in a minute. I just want to drop off some stuff on Drew's desk," Hero said, retreating to the computer room.

In Hero's absence, there was a quiet knock at the back door of the station.

Stealthily, and with no trouble walking at all, Samantha stole over to the door, opened it, and let Tyler in. In whispers, she explained how Drew was gone for the afternoon and Hero would be, too, as she had manipulated him into taking her home.

Tyler grinned. That would give him the time he needed to crack the ticket program.

Before Hero re-entered the room, Tyler had hidden himself away in one of the utility closets.

Samantha repositioned herself into a state of helplessness as Hero came back into the room. Without a second look at Samantha, Hero placed the printouts on Drew's desk and rapidly scribbled a note.

"Hero, my ankle's really beginning to throb. We better get going," Samantha called.

Hero parked his motorcycle at the curb in front of Samantha's house on Azalea Street, several blocks away from Amanda's house in the Cliffside Heights development.

Samantha swung her leg over the cycle and gingerly placed her foot on the ground, trying to stand.

"Oh, help," she whimpered. "Hero, I don't think I can put any weight on it at all now." She looked at him expectantly.

"Oh, all right, I'll carry you in," Hero said, exasperated.

Samantha slipped her arms around Hero's neck while he lifted her into his arms. Sighing, she leaned her head against his broad, strong chest.

Just as Hero entered Samantha's house, Amanda's white Mustang turned the corner onto Azalea Street.

Amanda and Kit were on their way to Cliffside Mall. Kit was, as usual, talking a mile a minute about sleepaway camp, the new friends she'd made, the pranks she'd pulled. She didn't care that Amanda just kept nodding and saying "Uh-huh." Kit was so glad that Amanda had promised to take her to the mall, Amanda didn't have to say a word.

"Hey, look at the cool motorcycle in front of Samantha's house," Kit said as they drove down Azalea Street. "Does Samantha have a new boyfriend?"

"Motorcycle!" Amanda exclaimed, snapping out of her reverie.

"Yeah—over there!" Kit said, pointing at the rebuilt Harley sitting in front of Samantha's house.

Without even having to stop and look, Amanda knew it was Hero's. Her face went white, and she felt like she'd been punched in the stomach.

"Oh, look, there he is now," Kit said, sticking her head out the window as Amanda sped up. "Hey, Amanda, why are you going so fast? I wanted to get a good look at him." Kit craned her neck to get a glimpse of Hero leaving Samantha's house.

"Who's the cute guy?" Kit asked, plopping back down on the seat.

"I wouldn't know," Amanda said, pressing her lips together.

"What do you mean you—"

"Kit, if you ask me one more question, I'm turning around and taking you right back home," Amanda said.

"Sheesh, what did I say?" Kit mumbled, giving Amanda a puzzled side glance.

Amanda stared straight ahead, eyes glistening with tears. She didn't know who or what to believe anymore. But one thing was clear: She was going to have it out with Hero once and for all.

Is this what it feels like when your heart's about to break? Amanda wondered, squeezing her eyes shut to hold back the tears.

Chapter Fourteen

*F*rom the moment Amanda had seen Hero leaving Samantha's house, she'd been working on automatic pilot. Samantha and Hero are together. That thought kept running through her brain as Amanda mechanically perused the clothing at The Rack, Kit's favorite store.

Dueling images kept replaying in Amanda's mind. There was Hero, indignantly telling her about Samantha's come-on. And there was Samantha's tear-streaked face, telling her about Hero. Who was she to believe? Who could she trust?

Amanda's eyes filled as she realized she'd lost her best friend and her boyfriend all in the same day.

Finally, after Kit had tried on everything in her size and purchased almost everything she had tried on, she was ready to go home.

During the car ride home, Amanda didn't say a word except to nod her assent as Kit chattered on. Kit stopped mid-sentence when she realized that Amanda wasn't even pretending to listen.

"Oh, and Amanda, you'll never believe this. I got married, and I'm pregnant, and I think I'm having twins. Can't you just see Mom and Dad as happy grand-parents?" Kit asked.

"Um-hmmmm," Amanda replied, just as she'd been doing all along.

Kit sighed.

"I'm going to drop you off at home, Kit," Amanda said into the yawning silence that filled the car.

"You know, Amanda, you haven't been listening to a word I've been saying. Come to think of it, you've been acting like a mannequin since we drove past Samantha's house and saw that guy coming out. Would you mind telling me what's going on?" Kit asked.

"Oh, Kit, you're too young. You wouldn't understand," Amanda said.

"Oh, really? Fine. Keep your ever-so-mature problems to yourself, then, and see if I care," Kit said, turning away from

140

Amanda to stare out the window.

Feeling like she didn't have a friendly soul in the world to talk to, Amanda reached over and lightly tapped Kit's arm.

"Hey, I'm sorry I said that. It's just . . ." Amanda drew in a shaky breath, unable to go on as tears filled her eyes.

Kit looked at Amanda in surprise. She'd never seen Amanda lose her cool like this before.

"Well," Amanda began again slowly. "You know that guy we saw coming out of Samantha's house?"

Kit nodded her head.

"That was Hero Montoya," Amanda said.

Kit's eyes grew round.

"You mean that's the guy Mom wrote me about—the guy you're so in love with?" she asked, incredulous. "What was he doing coming out of Samantha's house?" Seeing the pained look on Amanda's face, Kit hurriedly added, "I mean, I bet there's a really good explanation for why he was at Samantha's."

"If there is, I intend to find it out," Amanda said determinedly.

"How?" Kit wanted to know.

"After I drop you home, I'm going straight over to Samantha's and find out what is going on," Amanda told her.

"Why bother with Samantha? If it was me, I'd go talk to Hero. After all, Samantha's not likely to tell you the truth about anything, anyway," Kit said matter-of-factly.

Amanda looked at Kit in surprise. "What do you mean, Kit? Samantha's my best friend!"

"Hmmmmm. Some best friend," Kit said with a sniff. "In my young and immature opinion, Samantha spends half her life wanting to be like you and the other half trying to get what you have. I bet she talked Hero into coming over to her house just because he's *your* boyfriend."

"Kit! Why would you say something like that?" But Amanda had a niggling feeling that what Kit was saying might actually be true.

"Hey, don't listen to me. I'm just your thirteen-year-old sister. But I'm telling you, if I was going to trust somebody, it wouldn't be Samantha," Kit repeated.

Amanda didn't say another word until she pulled her Mustang alongside the curb in front of their house.

"Okay, little sister. Ride's over." After a short pause, Amanda added, "And thanks for the advice."

"Good luck," Kit said as she got out of the car, her arms filled with shopping bags.

"Thanks. Oh, and by the way, congratulations on your marriage and the twins. But no . . . I don't think Mom and Dad would be happy as grandparents," Amanda said with an impish grin. Kit's mouth opened wide in surprise as Amanda drove off.

Chapter Fifteen

*I*t had taken Tyler hours to break into the computer program Hero had set up. Tyler smiled fiendishly as he put the finishing touches on rerigging the input so that, for every call that came in, the ticket sales account would be reduced by double the amount of the caller's purchase.

Then he secured the change with a secret pass code. Hero and Drew couldn't change the program back even if they were smart enough to figure out what was going wrong, which Tyler sincerely doubted.

After all, Hero wasn't smart enough to figure out that it was Tyler who screwed up the oil tank on Hero's motorcycle the other day. And Drew still hadn't figured out that it was a Scott Enterprises subsidiary that had pulled the plug on the funds for Student KSS. Of course, no one at Scott Enterprises officially knew about this, since Tyler had pretended to be his father when he contacted accounting and rerouted those funds. Even so, Tyler knew this kind of subterfuge was way over Drew's head.

Tyler lounged back in his seat, arms crossed behind his head. He smiled with satisfaction as a ticket call came in, and he watched the account obediently debit itself on the computer screen.

With Hero occupied by Samantha and Student KSS at an end, Amanda would have no other distractions. Tyler happily contemplated how he would step in and fill the gap in Amanda's lonely heart.

The sound of the station door opening and closing sent Tyler into a flurry of motion. Hurriedly, he slipped out of the computer room and ducked into the washroom further down the hall. As Drew entered his office, Tyler appeared from the opposite end of the hallway.

"Hey, Tyler!" Drew greeted him with surprise. "You're working kind of late, aren't you?"

"Yeah, well, I just wanted to make sure I'd called every possible contributor,"

Tyler said with an uneasy grin. "There's only a few days before the concert, and I figure we need every cent," he added, unable to look Drew directly in the eye.

"That's the truth," Drew said, passing his hand over his forehead. "Well, thanks for your help, Tyler. We all really appreciate it."

"No problem, Drew. But I think I'm going to quit for tonight. I'll see you bright and early tomorrow," Tyler said as he headed for the door.

"Right," Drew said distractedly. He had just spotted the ticket sales printouts that Hero had left on his desk, and he was happily perusing the figures.

"All right! According to Hero's figures, we've got over $4,000 in ticket sales so far. We're getting there," Drew said.

Tyler left, grinning smugly. Drew wouldn't be so happy when he saw the ticket printouts the next day. And Tyler couldn't wait to see the expression on Hero's face when that day came.

Chapter Sixteen

*W*ith a backhanded wave to Kit, Amanda drove to the end of the block, heading for Azalea Street. But as Amanda drove along, she saw Samantha skip happily out of the house and hop into Tyler's father's Maserati. Remembering what Kit had said about Samantha, Amanda shifted gears and tore out, heading full speed toward Hero's house. She didn't have a clue what she was going to say.

As Amanda careened onto the street where Hero lived, she spied his motorcycle parked outside his house. Remembering the sight of Hero leaving Samantha's house made her angry all over again. Amanda swerved the car to a stop in front of the house, almost knocking over Hero's motorcycle, and jumped out.

Just as Amanda was about to knock,

Hero jerked open the door. Amanda and Hero stood face to face.

"Amanda—what—" Hero said, surprise and pleasure showing on his face at the same time.

"—am I doing here? Is that what you were going to ask? Were you expecting someone else, perhaps? Like Samantha?" Amanda asked angrily.

"Amanda, I'm surprised to see you. But why would I be expecting to see Samantha? What are you talking about?" Hero asked, genuinely puzzled.

"Oh, please. What's the point in pretending? Did you honestly think I wouldn't find out about the two of you? I can't believe you tried to convince me that she was after you when it was you after Samantha the whole time . . ." Amanda swallowed hard, unable to continue.

Hero went to take Amanda's shoulders in his hands, but she shot him such a fierce look that he stepped back, hands in the air.

"Whoa, hey, Amanda—slow down. Me after Samantha? Have you been out in the sun too long?" Hero asked in disbelief.

"Oh, so I suppose it wasn't you coming

150

out of Samantha's house this afternoon?" Amanda said accusingly.

A shadow passed over Hero's face. "Yeah, it was me, but—"

"I knew it. I knew you couldn't deny it," Amanda said, feeling like someone had stabbed her through the heart.

"What are you saying? You think I'm interested in Samantha and I've just been playing around with you to get to her?"

"I wouldn't know what you're planning," Amanda responded coolly. She stared at Hero as if she'd never seen him before in her life.

"Look, Amanda. Samantha fell and twisted her ankle at the station. Drew asked me to give her a ride home. That's the whole story," Hero said flatly.

Amanda was stunned by Hero's bald-faced lie. "I see. Well, in that case, there's nothing more to say," she snapped. Feeling totally betrayed, Amanda headed for her car.

"Amanda, what are you talking about?" Hero asked.

"Nothing. There's nothing left to talk about," Amanda said. "But, for your information, I saw Samantha not more than twenty minutes ago, and there was nothing wrong with her ankle."

"What?" Hero asked, astonished.

"Good-bye, Hero," Amanda said, trying not to let Hero see the tears that were beginning to fill her eyes.

"Amanda, wait . . . " Hero started to say. But his voice was lost amidst the noise of Amanda's car engine as she raced away from the sidewalk.

Amanda didn't know where she was going, but she knew she had to get away from Hero. She felt as if Hero had ripped out her heart and wrung it dry. How could she have been so stupid? How could she have loved him? Amanda wondered, sobbing against the wind as it whipped her hair against her face.

Without thinking, Amanda headed for Bluff Cove. It was where she and Samantha and Tyler used to go to tell each other secrets, although they hadn't all been there together in a very long time.

The cove overlooked the ocean and was hidden from the road. It had always been the perfect place to be alone in, or to hide. Amanda smiled as she remembered how, when she was ten years old, she'd run away from home. She'd gotten as far as the cove, with her backpack and her pillow, then lain down to rest, just for a minute, before she continued on her way. Her father had found her sleeping, curled up under the bluff—just in time, too. If she'd been there an hour longer, the tide would have carried her out.

Shaking her head sadly, Amanda knew that, this time, her father wasn't going to be able to rescue her and make everything all right. This time, she was completely on her own.

As Amanda drove along the dirt road that led to Bluff Cove, she noticed a familiar Maserati parked at the edge of the road. Oh, great. Samantha and Tyler are here, Amanda thought. Just the people she didn't want to run into.

Amanda was about to back down the road and head elsewhere, but she changed her mind. The cove was as good a place as any to have it out with Samantha once and for all. If Samantha's attraction to Hero was a surprise to Tyler, too, then so much the better, Amanda thought grimly.

Amanda stepped out of the car and headed for the footpath that led to the cove beneath the bluff. As Amanda walked carefully down the path, she could hear the murmur of Tyler's and Samantha's voices mingling with the sound of the waves lapping against the shore.

As Amanda rounded the bend, she heard them mention her name. Amanda paused. She didn't like the idea of eavesdropping. Still, Samantha *had* betrayed their friendship, and Amanda wasn't likely to get the truth from Samantha directly.

Quietly, Amanda crept closer to the edge of the cove. There she crouched, silent and unmoving, straining to hear what Samantha and Tyler had to say.

" . . . and Hero took me home on . . . and then I made him carry me into my house . . . he didn't want to, but . . . pretending my ankle . . . the whole time . . ." was all Amanda could hear. Then she heard the tinkle of Samantha's giggle and Tyler's sharp, raspy laugh.

Amanda bit her lip so hard it bled. Tears stung her eyes. Hero had been telling the truth!

Amanda didn't know what to do first. Should she confront Samantha? Should she race back to Hero and apologize?

". . . did you . . . your plan?"

Amanda held her breath. Tyler had a plan? About what?

"Don't worry about my end . . . all taken care of . . . Hero . . . concert . . . KSS . . . finished," was all Amanda could hear above the waves and the wind.

What does that mean—Hero, concert, KSS, finished? Amanda thought wildly to herself as she leaned back against the rocky wall of the cove.

"Tell me what . . . or maybe I'll let Amanda know . . ." Samantha threatened.

"You're in this as deep . . . asking for trouble . . . try to rat me out," Tyler replied nastily.

Amanda had heard enough. Quickly, she scrambled up the footpath, got into her car, and started up the engine. Amanda backed along the dirt road until it ended. Then she spun the car around, gravel spewing from under her tires. Flooring the accelerator, Amanda's car hit the highway at the speed limit.

"I'm coming, Hero. And I'm sorry," Amanda whispered.

Chapter Seventeen

The next day, Amanda burst into the studio bright and early, looking for Hero. The only thing on her mind was to find him and tell him she'd been wrong—completely and totally wrong. Amanda hadn't been able to get in touch with Hero at all yesterday. He hadn't been home when Amanda had raced to his house, and he hadn't returned any of her numerous phone calls.

Looking around, Amanda saw Hero deep in conversation with Drew behind the glass walls of his office. Jamar and Keera were uneasily hanging around the main office area.

"Hey, sorry I'm late. What's going on? Why are Hero and Drew closeted in Drew's office?" Amanda asked breathlessly.

"Well, with only one day left before the

concert, it turns out there's a problem with the ticket sales," Keera said unhappily.

"What do you mean?" Amanda asked.

"Drew went over Hero's tally sheet last night, and it turns out we've got less than $2,000 in the ticket till," Jamar explained.

"How can that be?" Amanda asked. "Just yesterday Hero said we had almost $4,000."

Jamar and Keera exchanged uneasy glances.

"Well, that's what he and Drew are talking about—" Keera started to say.

Suddenly, an idea took hold in Amanda's mind. Interrupting Keera, she asked, "Have Tyler and Samantha come in today?"

Jamar shifted uncomfortably in his chair. "As a matter of fact, they were here just a few minutes ago. You just missed them and . . ." Jamar's voice trailed off.

"And . . ." Amanda prompted him.

"They were here when Drew noticed that the tally sheet Hero had left yesterday didn't match the tally sheet that Drew printed out this morning," Keera reluctantly explained.

"And . . ." Amanda said again, her eyes narrowing with suspicion.

"And Tyler insinuated that Hero took some of the money off the top to finance his cycle repairs," Jamar finished for her.

Amanda gasped.

"And before either of us could say anything, Samantha suggested that maybe something had gone wrong with the computer program. That drove Hero even further out of his mind than Tyler's comment," Keera told her. "Then Drew stepped in and asked Hero to come into his office."

"And that's when Tyler and Samantha split, I bet," Amanda said.

Jamar nodded his head.

"What's on your mind, Amanda?" Keera asked, seeing that something was brewing behind those violet eyes.

Before Amanda could tell Keera what she'd heard yesterday at Bluff Cove, Hero exploded out of Drew's office like a heat-seeking missile. Eyes blazing, Hero blew past them.

"Hero, wait!" Amanda called anxiously.

Hero ignored Amanda. Throwing on his leather jacket, he flung himself out the door.

Stunned by the fury of Hero's exit, no one moved for a moment. Then Amanda ran to open the door to follow Hero. But by that time, all she could see was a cloud of dust as Hero's motorcycle zoomed out of sight.

Amanda was torn. Should she follow Hero in her car? Should she hunt down Samantha and Tyler and confront them? Looking back inside the station, Amanda saw Drew standing in the doorway of his office, holding the two printouts and looking grim.

I'll tell Drew. He'll know what to do, Amanda decided.

"Drew, we have to talk," Amanda said. "I think I know what happened."

"Anything that would shed some light on this situation would be greatly appreciated," Drew said gravely. "Hero hasn't been able to account for the missing money—and frankly, neither have I."

"Oh, Drew, you can't possibly think . . ." Keera started to say.

"I don't know what to think," Drew said unhappily.

"I'm absolutely positive that Hero didn't have anything to do with the missing money," Amanda said.

"No one would expect you to say anything different," Drew said gently.

"I'm not saying this because Hero and I

are together." Amanda faltered for a moment, her eyes glistening with tears. "I mean, we're not together anymore, because I screwed it all up, but that's not the point. I overheard Samantha and Tyler talking yesterday, when they thought they were alone. I could only hear every other word, but I heard enough to know that Tyler has to be responsible for the missing money," Amanda said in a rush.

"Come on, Amanda—how could Tyler be responsible? He didn't have anything to do with the ticketing," Drew said. "And he surely doesn't need the money," he added wryly. "In fact, he was working late by himself here just last night . . . " Drew's voice trailed off, as he remembered Tyler's awkward departure the previous evening.

"I knew it," Amanda said excitedly. "I'm telling you, I overheard Tyler say something about Hero and KSS being finished for good. I just know that he's responsible somehow. Maybe Tyler changed the programming or deleted the money. Tyler's good at figuring out computer stuff—he's been playing with the computers at his Dad's business for as long as I can remember."

"Drew, man, we owe it to Hero to at least check out the possibility of foul play," Jamar spoke up.

"You're right, we do," Drew said. "Amanda, I'm going to run through the programming on the computer. See if you can find Tyler. If you're right, he's going to have a lot of explaining to do."

"What can we do?" Keera asked quietly.

"Somebody ought to look for Hero," Amanda said, "and get him to come back so we can straighten out this whole mess."

"Shouldn't that be you?" Keera asked Amanda.

Amanda shook her head. "I've really messed things up between Hero and me," Amanda said unhappily. "I don't think he'd even listen to me."

"Okay, then," Jamar said decisively. "Keera and I will scope out Hero. Amanda, you find Tyler. Let's agree to meet back here in, say, three hours."

"Done," Amanda said solemnly.

"Later," Jamar called, leading a reluctant Keera out the door.

Chapter Eighteen

*W*hile Keera drove, she glanced sideways at Jamar. He was studiously looking out the window, checking for any sign of Hero or Hero's motorcycle.

Keera still hadn't had the opportunity to tell Jamar that she thought it would be best if they broke up. She hadn't told him how tired she was of his obsession with Rogue, the band, and his music, and how she couldn't stand coming last in his life. If he couldn't find time for her, well, then she didn't have time for him either. Every time she tried to say it, the words stuck in her throat and Jamar ended up holding her, like the other day at her house.

Keera's mother's words resounded in her head.

"You're better off without any scatter-brained musicians, honey. You need to focus on the SATs, so you can go to

Stanford or someplace like that—like your brother Malcolm."

But I think I really love him, Keera had wanted to say to her mother. And I think he really loves me. Sometimes he can be so sweet, so full of fun.

But the look on her mother's face prevented Keera from saying any of those things.

Suddenly, sitting next to Jamar, she was able to remember only the good times they'd had over the past month.

Like the time, right after the Beach Bash, when Jamar surprised her and took her to see Shakespeare in the Arborium because she loved the play *A Midsummer Night's Dream*—even though he hadn't a clue what was going on.

Keera melted inside at the memory of how they'd held each other close, watching the performance, Jamar's arms surrounding hers, his lips softly nuzzling the nape of her neck, raising goose bumps up and down her body despite the warmth of the early evening air.

Or the time when he'd taken her with him on one of his solo Saturday night gigs at Dancer's Roadhouse, twenty miles past the county line. Keera had never been to any place like that before. She smiled, thinking how horrified her mother would have been if she'd known that Jamar had brought Keera there.

The place was dark and smoky, and it smelled like hay. But, when Jamar played, Keera closed her eyes and imagined that he was playing just for her—with no one else around. Keera could still feel the cool sea breeze that washed over them as they walked on the cliffs along the shore after the gig. Moonlight had glistened on the ocean, reflecting in Jamar's shining eyes.

Keera sighed with pleasure at the memory of Jamar's warm hands on the smooth, cool skin of her face as he gently brought her mouth up to his, tenderly covering her lips with his own and murmuring how much he loved her. Keera didn't know if she'd shuddered from excitement or from the cold. Whatever the reason, Jamar had brought her to him, holding her closer, and closer, until she no longer knew where he ended and she began.

Her thoughts were interrupted by the crackling sound of static as Jamar fiddled with the station wagon's antiquated radio.

She looked over at him again, and Jamar smiled his crinkly smile, which always brought a responding smile to Keera's lips.

"You know, Keera," Jamar said softly, "I've been trying to tell you something really special for a while now, but I just haven't had the chance."

Keera waited, breathless. Was he going to tell her how much he loved her, as he had that night along the cliff? Would he say that nothing—not his music, his friends, his band—nothing but Keera mattered? What was she going to do if he said that? With all her heart and soul, Keera wanted Jamar to love her and to spend all of his time with her. But, even as she wished that, she wondered where that would leave her schoolwork—and her promise to her parents to study and work as hard as she could.

"I just want you to know that I think this is going to be the most important thing that has ever happened to me in my whole life," Jamar began solemnly, his eyes twinkling.

Keera held her breath, waiting expectantly for what Jamar was about to say.

"Rogue and I worked out this cool deal for JellyJam for the concert . . ." Jamar began. The words tumbled out in his excitement to tell her about the song he had written for her, and that JellyJam and Grim Reaper would perform it together. In fact, Nick Ganos and Grim Reaper were coming to Jamar's garage tonight to rehearse!

But as soon as Keera heard the words "Rogue" and "JellyJam," she stopped listening, and her smile froze on her lips. All the reasons she'd wanted to break up with Jamar in the first place flooded through her.

"Maybe it would be better if you looked for Hero by yourself," Keera interrupted.

"What? What are you talking about? Did you hear what I said?" Jamar asked her incredulously.

"Uh-huh. I heard you talking about Rogue, and JellyJam, and the concert—like you always do," Keera responded. "And I think what we should be doing right now is looking for Hero, not talking about your usual obsessions. The best way to do that is to spread out—separate. You take the trail roads along the beach on your bicycle, I'll keep going on the streets." Keera stopped the car alongside Cliffside Beach.

Jamar shook his head in puzzlement. "I just don't understand you, girlfriend. Here I'm trying to tell you . . ."

Jamar stopped, seeing the closed expression on Keera's face. "Aw, forget it," he said with disgust, yanking open the car door. He pulled his bicycle from the trunk of the car where he'd stashed it when they'd set out on their search for Hero. With one long, tragic look back at Keera, Jamar pedaled off.

Keera stared straight ahead, not trusting herself to return Jamar's look. After a few moments, she turned her head to watch Jamar's departing back as he disappeared along the trail. Keera didn't know whether she wanted to cry or sigh in relief.

My life was perfectly fine before Jamar was in it. And it will be perfectly fine without him, Keera told herself fiercely. He's not the only one with a busy life. After the concert, I'm going to tell him we're totally through.

Chapter Nineteen

*S*everal hours later, Amanda drove back to the KSS-TV station. She hadn't had any luck finding Tyler, and she was feeling very frustrated. As she stepped through the doorway of the station, Amanda tripped on a heavy, sealed manila envelope lying on the floor.

Amanda picked it up. She gasped when she saw Drew's name printed in familiar bold, sloping handwriting. Squeezing the contents to figure out what was inside, Amanda walked slowly into Drew's office. A queasy feeling was forming in the pit of her stomach.

Silently, Amanda held the envelope out to Drew.

"What's this?" Drew asked, surprised.

"I'm not sure. I found it on the floor near the door. I think it's from Hero," Amanda said quietly.

Drew hurriedly ripped open the envelope. Out fell a slip of paper. It read, simply, "I'm sorry." Several packets of twenty-dollar bills were also in the envelope. Drew quickly totaled the cash.

"There's $2,400 in here," Drew said in a hushed tone.

"Where would Hero get that kind of money?" Amanda asked, incredulous.

"Maybe there was something to what Tyler said after all," Drew began to say.

"I don't believe it," Amanda declared. "I just don't believe that Hero would steal money from anyone, much less from the KSS-Off fund."

"Well, I've been through the computer program a lot of times. I can't figure out why it's subtracting money instead of adding it, and I can't tell where the money is going instead. And here's a note saying he's sorry . . . and he obviously doesn't want to face us . . ." Drew shook his head unhappily. "I never would have figured Hero for being dishonest."

"I'm telling you, I'm sure there's some other explanation," Amanda insisted. "And this time I'm going to find out what it is."

Amanda flung herself out of the station, bumping into Jamar on his way in.

"Amanda, what's up?" Jamar asked as Amanda streaked by him.

"Did you find Hero?" Amanda asked over her shoulder, sure that the answer was no.

"No, but—where are you going?" Jamar asked.

"To find out the truth," Amanda called back as she slammed into her car.

Amanda clutched the steering wheel of her Mustang until her knuckles were white and her fingers ached. She watched the streets, hoping to catch a glimpse of Hero's leather-clad form or hear the roar of his motorcycle. Before long, Amanda found herself driving down Hero's street. She pulled up to his house and turned into the driveway.

Amanda's heart jumped when, in the fading light, she saw a form move quickly behind the window shade. Amanda looked around for Hero's motorcycle, but it wasn't there. Neither was Hero's mother's old Buick.

Amanda ran up to the front door and rang the bell. Nobody answered. Amanda listened at the door, but all was dark and still inside.

On the other side of the door, Hero held his breath, not daring to move a muscle. The last thing he wanted right now was to have to face Amanda. Giving Drew that $2,400 was the hardest thing Hero had ever done in his life. He definitely wasn't up to explaining to Amanda how he got it .

Amanda knocked one last time, then slowly drew away from the front door in defeat. How was she ever going to be able to set things right if she couldn't find Hero? An unbidden tear slipped out the corner of her eye and rolled down her cheek.

Watching Amanda's departing back through a crack in the door, Hero had no idea how things had gotten so out of hand. How was he going to be able to face everyone at the concert tomorrow? Yet how could he stay home and let everyone down again? Hero sank down on his heels, his back against the wall, his head held despairingly in his hands.

Slowly, Amanda got back into her car. She couldn't escape the nagging feeling that someone was home at Hero's house. But of course, that was ridiculous. No one had answered the door, and Hero's motorcycle wasn't anywhere around.

As Amanda headed for home, she thought again about what she'd over-heard between Samantha and Tyler. Knowing she wasn't likely to get hold of Tyler if he didn't want to be found, Amanda decided it was time to confront Samantha.

Amanda turned onto Azalea Street. Samantha's car was by the curb, so Amanda knew she was home. With leaden feet, Amanda slowly trekked up the walk to the front door, remembering the hundreds of times she'd eagerly skipped up this path, anxious to tell all to Samantha about some excitement or another and to hear all about Samantha's escapades as well.

Suddenly, the image of Samantha's solemn, twelve-year-old face swearing to Amanda that they must never let a boy come between them came unbidden into Amanda's mind. Amanda remembered her own solemn promise back. Her face burned as she thought how Samantha had shamelessly reminded Amanda of that oath the other day and then gone right ahead and broken it.

Lost in thought, Amanda was startled when Samantha opened the door before she'd even had a chance to ring the bell. "Hey, Amanda," Samantha said in a bright and friendly tone. "I was just on my way over to the Snack Shack. Want to come?"

"Are you meeting Tyler there?" Amanda asked.

"No, why would I be meeting Tyler?"

"Oh, I just wondered," Amanda said. "So, I guess you know about Hero and the ticket money," she added.

"I know—it's a real shame. I still can't believe he'd do something like that," Samantha responded uneasily.

"Me either," Amanda said with a casual shrug. "But I guess you never can tell about a person, no matter how well you think you know him . . . or her," Amanda added pointedly.

"What do you mean, 'her'?" Samantha asked.

"Oh, I just mean, you never can tell about someone. Even if she's a really close friend, she could just decide one day to stab you in the back for no apparent reason," Amanda continued, keeping her voice light and even.

"Just what are you trying to say, Amanda?" Samantha asked. Her blue eyes darted all around, refusing to meet Amanda's violet ones.

Amanda couldn't contain herself any longer. "You lied to me about Hero, Samantha. Hero wasn't coming on to you—you were the one who came on to him. And now you and Tyler are mixed up in some scheme to make him look like he stole the money from the ticket fund."

"I don't know what you're talking about, Amanda Townsend," Samantha retorted indignantly.

"Oh, really? Then I suppose that wasn't you at Bluff Cove with Tyler yesterday, talking about some evil plan to ruin Hero, the concert, and KSS?" Amanda flung the words in Samantha's face.

Samantha's expression changed from outrage to total guilt. "You heard us talking at Bluff Cove?" Samantha said, her face pale.

"Yes, I did, so there's no point in trying to deny it."

Samantha looked away. "Amanda, I really didn't know that Tyler was planning to make it look like Hero stole the ticket money," she said contritely.

"So, I'm right—Tyler did do something to the computer program. And you're telling me you didn't have anything to do with that? Am I supposed to believe you after you lied to me about Hero asking you out? You tried to break up Hero and me so that *you* could have him for yourself!" Amanda said contemptuously.

Amanda said nothing, waiting for Samantha to continue.

"Look, it's true, I did try to get between you and Hero. I was jealous of the way you looked so happy together, and I just thought that if I could get Hero's attention, maybe Tyler would finally notice me instead of only thinking about you," Samantha tried to explain.

"Tyler? This is about you wanting to go out with Tyler?" Amanda asked in disbelief.

"I know, it sounds ridiculous. Tyler doesn't even know that I'm alive, except when he's thinking about how I can help him get *you* to go out with him. I just figured that, if I helped Tyler, and showed him that Hero could like me, maybe he'd be jealous and finally want *me*!" Samantha wailed.

Amanda looked at Samantha pityingly. How could she have thought that Samantha was her friend? Pushing her own feelings of betrayal and hurt aside, Amanda decided it was time to take action.

"You're coming with me, now," Amanda said, firmly clasping Samantha's wrist and leading her to the Mustang.

"Where are we going?" Samantha asked tearfully, allowing herself to be pulled along.

"We're going back to the station to explain this to Drew. Then we're going to try to find Hero, before he does anything really crazy . . ." Amanda gasped, remembering the packets of money. Where in the world could Hero have come up with that kind of cash?

Suddenly, it hit Amanda. Hero had sold his motorcycle!

Amanda and Samantha burst into the KSS station and raced into Drew's office.

The station manager was just hanging up the telephone with a deeply puzzled expression on his face.

"Drew, Samantha has something to tell you. It wasn't Hero after all, and I think he sold his motorcycle," Amanda blurted.

"Whoa, slow down. What are you talking about? What is it that you have to say, Samantha?" Drew asked.

Amanda nudged Samantha toward Drew's desk.

"Well . . ." Samantha started to say slowly.

"Come on, Samantha, there isn't a whole lot of time," Amanda said impatiently.

Taking a deep breath, Samantha began again. "I think that Tyler somehow deleted the ticket money on the computer. Hero definitely didn't have anything to do with it, and *I* had no idea that Tyler was going to take the ticket money and blame Hero—honest. I was just supposed to keep Hero busy while Tyler messed around with the computer. It was all supposed to be a big trick on Hero, and a way for me to get back at Amanda for being so totally perfect all the time. I never dreamed everything would get so serious. And that's the total, honest truth, I swear."

"That still doesn't explain why Hero left $2,400 in cash on our doorstep, nor does it explain where he got it," Drew said, looking at Amanda.

"That's what I was trying to tell you just a moment ago," Amanda said, exasperated. "I think Hero sold his motorcycle to come up with the difference in the ticket money."

Drew looked very solemn. "If what you're telling me is true, then this telephone call I just had and your information give me two good reasons to call Tyler Scott, Senior."

"What do you mean?" Amanda asked.

"Well, it turns out that the reason our student funding got dropped was because TST, Inc., a subsidiary of Scott Enterprises which donates money to non-profit organizations, was told by the main accounting department at Scott Enterprises to stop all donations to KSS.

"The only thing is, no one at Scott Enterprises knows where the order to stop the donations came from. And no one knows anyone by the name of Roger Herkimer, the 'Vice-President' who signed that letter I showed you last Saturday, telling us that Student KSS was juvenile and amateurish," Drew finished.

Amanda and Samantha looked at each other. "Tyler!" they said together.

"But how could Tyler . . .?" Drew left his question unfinished.

"I told you Tyler's been working on his father's computer systems since he could read," Amanda said, trembling with anger. "I bet he maneuvered this whole thing to wreck KSS and wreck our jobs. And then, when we decided to put on the KSS-Off Concert, he had to make sure we weren't able to raise enough money to keep going!"

"That's a pretty serious accusation, Amanda," Drew said slowly.

"Well, there's one way to find out if it's true," Amanda said, handing the telephone to Drew. "Call up Mr. Scott, and see what he has to say. In the meantime, I'm going to try to find Hero. Come on, Samantha, you've still got a lot of explaining to do."

Chapter Twenty

*A*fter driving around for what seemed like hours, Keera finally gave up. Hero obviously didn't want to be found. Stopping at a pay phone, Keera called Drew to report, telling him that she was heading for home instead of returning to the station. She couldn't bear the thought of facing Jamar yet again today.

For the rest of the afternoon and early evening, Keera holed up in her room, staring at her SAT practice tests, trying desperately to concentrate. But the little fill-in circles kept swimming before her eyes as tears trickled down her cheeks.

Keera gazed half-heartedly out the window, watching the sun sink lower and lower in the sky. She wished with all her heart that things had worked out with Jamar. For a minute she pretended that they were sitting on the sand, the waves lapping gently at their toes, watching the sun set over the ocean.

"Yes!" Akim shouted, breaking into Keera's reverie as he sank a basket in the driveway. For a moment, Keera almost expected to hear Jamar saying "My man!" in reply. When the phone rang, Keera jumped up, half-expecting that it would be Jamar. But no one called her to the phone.

At dinner, Keera could only pick at her food. "What's wrong, honey?" her father asked gently. "Are you starting to get nervous about the SAT? Are they working you too hard, preparing for the concert tomorrow?"

"Of course they're working her too hard about that fool concert," Mrs. Johnson replied. "I, for one, will be glad when it's all over. But I told you, Keera, it might be just as well if you take a break from that KSS job. Without the pressure of work, and now that you broke up with that Jamar boy, you'll be able to spend more time studying. Then you won't have to be nervous at all about that SAT test."

"You broke up with Jamar?" Mr.

182

Johnson asked with surprise. "I didn't know that."

"Oh, she broke up with him over a week ago, didn't you, honey?" Mrs. Johnson asked matter-of-factly.

Keera nodded.

"That's too bad. I kind of liked that boy," Mr. Johnson added, helping himself to more peas.

"Oh, he was the total opposite of Keera. What would she want with a fool-headed musician who'll never amount to anything?"

"Well, now, madam, you know what they say—opposites attract," Mr. Johnson said with a mischievous grin and a wink.

"Mama, what does 'broke up' mean?" Akim wanted to know.

"It means Keera told Jamar she doesn't want him bothering her, coming over here, taking up her time, keeping her from studying," Mrs. Johnson said.

"Does that mean Jamar isn't going to be playing basketball with me anymore?" Akim asked, crestfallen.

That was all Keera could stand. Abruptly, she pushed back her chair.

"I'm going out for a while, Mom. Do

you mind if I borrow the car?" Keera asked, not waiting for a reply. Scooping up the car keys she slipped out of the house.

Driving around, Keera could barely concentrate on where she was going. She was ashamed that she had lied to her mother, telling her that she'd already broken up with Jamar when she really hadn't. But there was no way she could explain to her mother how hard breaking up was to do.

Keera stopped the car along the beach and got out to think. The sea breeze tossed her curls and cooled her warm, flushed skin. She looked out to sea, hoping that the right words for what she had to do would magically drift over the current and float into her brain.

All of a sudden, Keera realized that there was never going to be an easy way to end this thing with Jamar.

How could she tell someone she was in love with—someone that she *thought* she was in love with—that he was just not right for her? She wished she had a book or something she could read to find out exactly what to do, what to say, Keera thought in despair.

Just then Keera's attention was caught by two sea gulls, swooping low over the ocean, hanging in the air together, the moon reflecting off the white tips of their wings.

Without warning, one gull dove into the water to catch a fish and the other simply flew off in the opposite direction.

In that moment, Keera knew what she had to do. It was stupid to wait until tomorrow, after the concert, to tell Jamar good-bye. She had to do it now—right this minute.

With tears streaming down her face, Keera drove over to Jamar's house. She was surprised by the number of cars, a black van, and several pick-up trucks that were parked up and down the street. Keera had to park all the way at the end of the block. As she strode toward Jamar's house, she could hear rock music resounding from his garage.

Keera slowed her pace. The music sounded like something of JellyJam's but there was more . . . more instruments, more something . . . she couldn't identify.

Then she noticed that the black van, suspended high off the ground on four oversized wheels, had multiple antennae sticking out all over the roof, and on its side, painted in a heavy white outline, a hooded figure holding a scythe. The same symbol was on practically all of the other cars and trucks.

Suddenly, it hit her. Grim Reaper was here! Nick Ganos was actually in Jamar's garage, playing with him and JellyJam—right here, right now!

In a flash, Keera realized *this* must have been what Jamar had been trying to tell her about before she had practically thrown him out of her car. Her cheeks flushed at how insensitive and unfeeling she had been.

Tentatively, Keera approached the garage door. She was beginning to consider the possibility that maybe Jamar wasn't the selfish, obsessive, Rogue-driven creature she had thought he was.

The loud, rolling music gave way to a softer, smokier sound. Crooning along with the music was—a voice Keera couldn't identify right away. It wasn't Rogue, it wasn't Nick Ganos. As the voice wafted out onto the street, with a chorus of voices singing behind it, Keera heard her name.

"Keera in my heart. . . Keera on my mind . . . the sea-foam in your eyes. . . leave my world behind. . . Keera on my mind. . . Love you always, all the time. . . Keera mine." The voice faded away as the song ended.

That's Jamar—singing a song about me! Keera gasped. Her mind reeled with the knowledge that Jamar really did love her. His music and his friends weren't more important than she was, after all.

She couldn't believe how wrong she was—and how totally stupid. Keera groaned inwardly.

"I've got to tell you, man," Keera heard Nick Ganos's gruff voice say, "that is one helluva song. After this gig tomorrow, I want to talk to you some more about performing it on my tour, okay?"

"Sure, man," Jamar responded, sounding uncharacteristically down.

Then Keera heard Rogue step in and take over. "The Jammin' man here means definitely, Nick, definitely. We'd love to talk to you about doing the song. We'll see you tomorrow then—and thanks a lot for coming by."

Keera stepped back into the shadows as

the garage door opened and Nick Ganos, the Grim Reapers, and JellyJam filed out, packed up their equipment, and left in their assorted vehicles, amidst parting calls of "Later," and "Tomorrow!"

Standing in the driveway, watching the last Reaper vehicle drive away, Rogue turned to Jamar and slapped him on the side of the head.

"What is with you, dude, saying 'sure' like Nick Ganos just offered you a stick of gum? The man wants to do your song. Nick Ganos of Grim Reaper wants to perform *your* song! Do you get that?" Rogue shouted.

Jamar turned to Rogue. "Yeah, man, I get it. So, I've got a great song—but no Keera. She won't even listen to me or talk to me anymore. She threw me out of her car this afternoon. Her mother says she doesn't want to come to the phone to talk to me. I'm practically going out of my mind because the one person I love most in the world doesn't give a damn about me—so, excuse me if I'm not exactly up to your level of enthusiasm."

Keera's eyes opened wide. Jamar loved her! And he cared more about her than what should have been the biggest moment of his life!

Keera's eyes glittered angrily when she realized that her mother had been screening her calls and not even telling her that Jamar had been on the phone!

"Oh, come on, dude. You're better off without that bookworm. Nick Ganos wants to perform your song. We're going places, man—we're going to be somebody. You'll be able to get a million girls, a lot better looking and a lot more fun than Keera Johnson," Rogue said contemptuously.

Keera flushed with anger and mortification. She was just about to step out of the shadows when she heard the sound of a fist landing across Rogue's jaw. Rogue sprawled on the ground, rubbing his face with his hand, looking totally surprised.

"That's the last time I want to hear you say Keera's name," Jamar said coldly. "After tomorrow's concert, I'm pulling out of the band."

Then Jamar turned on his heel, went back into the garage, and pulled down the door, leaving Rogue to scramble up from where Jamar had dropped him.

Angrily, Rogue brushed himself off. He was about to climb into his Jeep when he noticed Keera in the shadows.

"So, you got what you wanted, didn't you?" Rogue snarled at her. "Enter Keera, exit Rogue, exit JellyJam, exit everything we've been working for. Isn't that what you wanted?"

Then, before Keera could reply, Rogue flung himself into the Jeep and took off.

Keera stood motionless in the driveway. He'd done it. Jamar had actually done it—thrown it all away. Over her. Keera couldn't believe it.

Now there was something Keera had to do. And there was no putting it off until tomorrow.

Jamar's eyes went wide with surprise when he opened the door and saw Keera standing there..

"Wait! Don't say a thing. Not a word," Keera told him firmly. "There's something I have to do, and I don't want you to keep me from doing it."

Keera wrapped her arms around Jamar's neck, gently pulled his head down to hers, and kissed him slowly and languidly, full on the mouth. Her lips expressed all the love she felt for him.

Grateful and happy, Jamar took Keera in his arms and held her close, murmuring her name over and over, just as he had in the song.

Chapter Twenty-One

"*W*here are we, Amanda?" Samantha asked suspiciously. "Whose house is this, anyway?"

"You'll see," Amanda said shortly. She pressed her finger firmly on the doorbell. For several minutes no one answered, although Amanda saw someone lift the kitchen curtain ever so slightly to peer out. Refusing to give up, Amanda pressed the buzzer again.

Finally, the door opened, Amanda was all set to rush in and apologize to Hero. But to her surprise, it was Mrs. Montoya who stood in the doorway. She gazed coolly at the two girls on her doorstep.

"May I help you?" Mrs. Montoya asked politely.

"Oh, yes, Mrs. Montoya—I'm Amanda, Amanda Townsend. And this is Samantha Walker. I've always wanted to meet you, but Hero never . . . Well, that's not important now. Is Hero home? We really need to speak with him."

"I'm sorry, Amanda," Mrs. Montoya said. "My son isn't here right now, but I'll tell him you stopped by."

Although she didn't want to appear rude, Amanda couldn't help trying to peer around Mrs. Montoya's body into the darkened house.

"Oh. I was really hoping he was here, because Samantha . . . I mean we all made a terrible mistake, and I wanted to apologize to him for being such a jerk."

For a moment, Mrs. Montoya's eyes softened at the sorrow on Amanda's pretty face. But then she remembered the hurt look on Hero's face when he told her about what had happened, and how he had sold his motorcycle. Then, it was easy for Mrs. Montoya to harden her heart against these rich girls who thought they could play with her son's emotions.

"I'm sorry, Amanda, Samantha. I'll let Hero know you stopped by," Mrs. Montoya repeated.

Then, before Amanda could say another thing, Mrs. Montoya slipped back inside the house and quietly closed the door, leaving Amanda and Samantha standing out on the tiny porch.

Amanda and Samantha rode back to Samantha's house in silence. Occasionally, Samantha glanced over at Amanda, started to speak, and then thought better of it. When Amanda pulled up in front of Samantha's house on Azalea Street, she turned to Samantha and said calmly, "Good-bye, Samantha."

"Oh, Amanda, I'm so . . ." Samantha began to say, but Amanda cut her off with one swift glare.

"I've got nothing to say to you, Samantha. And there's nothing you could say that I would want to hear. Good-bye, Samantha," Amanda repeated firmly.

With a heavy sigh, Samantha stepped out of Amanda's car. She gave Amanda one last regretful look, then ran into the house.

Amanda, who had been holding back her tears since she'd driven away from the Montoya house, put her head down on the steering wheel and started to weep. She'd lost Hero, she'd lost Samantha, and in all probability she was going to lose her KSS job as well.

Just last week, Amanda had thought this was turning out to be the best summer of her life. At this moment, it felt like the very worst.

Chapter Twenty-Two

*I*t was Saturday afternoon, the day of the KSS-Off Concert. When Amanda arrived at Cliffside Park, it was a mass of electronic equipment, trucks, and guys in work clothes looking for places to put things down. Keera was in the middle of it all, her curls practically sticking out from tension and excitement.

"I'm glad you're here," Keera told Amanda with relief. "Would you tell those guys where to put that electronic equipment? I haven't the faintest idea. I'm trying to get the food and drink guys set up, and now they're telling me they need to be near an outlet. Where am I supposed to find an outlet in the park?"

"Calm down. I told the electric company to bring an extra generator. Once we get going, I'll send them over and you can get the food stands on it. It's okay, Keera," Amanda said calmly.

But Keera continued her nervous tirade as if Amanda hadn't said anything at all. "And Hero's supposed to be setting up a box office at the park entrance, but he isn't here . . ." Keera's voice trailed off as she realized that she had inadvertently struck a nerve.

"Have you heard from Hero?" Keera asked.

"No," Amanda replied stiffly. "I tried all last night, and I mean *all*. He obviously doesn't want anything to do with us—with me, I guess."

Keera gave Amanda a quick hug. "He'll show up. I know he will," she said. "Tickets don't go on sale until 3:00, and it's only 1:30 now. Don't mind me, I'm just a little jittery about the concert. Hero *will* show up, Amanda," Keera repeated.

"I hope so, Keera. Do you know about Tyler and Samantha?"

"I do. Drew told me," Keera said. Quickly changing the subject, she added, "Speaking of Drew, I can't figure out what's taking him so long to get here. He was on some kind of major conference call when I stopped by the station, but I thought he'd be done with it and here by now."

"Oh, you know Drew. He's always on the phone, and he's always late for everything," Amanda said. "So, before we get too busy to talk, what's the final performance schedule?" Amanda felt a little out of touch. After spending all day yesterday looking for Hero and all night trying to call him, she wasn't exactly on top of all the concert details.

"JellyJam is scheduled to go on first, then Jezebels, and then Nick Ganos and Grim Reaper. JellyJam and Grim Reaper are going to do an ensemble finale. They're going to perform this new song that Jamar wrote," Keera told Amanda, her eyes shining.

"You're kidding. That's fabulous! Have you heard the song yet?" Amanda wanted to know.

"I have," Keera said shyly.

Amanda examined Keera's face. "It's a song for you, isn't it?" Amanda guessed.

"It is," Keera replied, grinning.

"That is so romantic," Amanda exclaimed. Then she sighed. There was nothing like that in her future, that was for sure.

"And Jamar?" Amanda asked.

Keera blushed. "He's fine. He's great. We're great, too, now."

Smiling, Amanda said, "I'm glad. But I meant, when is he coming?"

Keera blushed even more furiously. "Oh, right, he's coming soon. JellyJam will be here at 2:30, and Nick Ganos and Jamie West are coming around 6:30. Jamar asked us to meet them at the south entrance so they don't get swamped on their way to the bandstand. We don't go on the air until 6:00, but we're on the air till 10:00, and the three bands are going to alternate sets till we go off."

"Sounds good," Amanda murmured. But she looked sad.

Seeing Amanda's forlorn look, Keera put her arm around Amanda's shoulders.

"He'll be here, Amanda," Keera said gently.

Yes, but would he ever speak to her again? Amanda asked herself. Shaking off her sadness, Amanda squared her shoulders and said, "I'm fine. Come on, we've got a concert to run."

At 2:30, Hero stood outside the hastily

erected police barricades that cordoned off the area of the park where the concert was being held.

He felt truly guilty, seeing how much work the others had done setting up the bandstand, the electrical wiring, the cameras, and the food stands. But his guilt wasn't enough to make him show up one second earlier than he had to, to help with the ticketing.

Going over to the park rangers, who were on call today to help handle the crowds, Hero explained who he was, and they allowed him through to the makeshift box office cabin that the park used for concerts.

"Hey, you're Hero Montoya," the young park ranger who was manning the ticket booth said with a grin. "Drew Pearson said you'd be by. Love your show."

"Thanks," Hero replied. "How are sales?" he asked, changing the subject.

"Doing pretty well, I'd say," the ranger said amiably, holding up a strongbox stuffed with receipts. "Ready to take over for a while?" he asked.

"Sure," Hero agreed, glad to have something to do.

When Amanda spotted Hero, her heart nearly burst with relief. He was here. She would be able to speak to him, to apologize. Then maybe everything could go back to the way it was before. Excusing herself from an argument between a lighting man and a sound technician, Amanda walked quickly over to Hero.

From the corner of his eye, Hero caught Amanda heading toward him. Hero didn't want to talk to her. He didn't want to have anything to do with her. Her lack of trust had hurt him deeper than anyone he'd ever known. No, he was definitely not going to talk to her, he vowed to himself. Not now, not ever.

To avoid facing Amanda, Hero decided to open for business immediately. As the crowd started shuffling past, kids greeted him and wished him luck. Once inside, people fanned out over the vast expanse of the Cliffside Park lawns to find a perfect spot from which to watch the concert.

"Hero," Amanda called, trying to get his attention as she fought against the flood of bodies. She had the surreal feeling that she was having a bad dream. Hero would not turn around.

Just then, Amanda saw Drew arrive at the ticket booth. Drew pulled the crinkled envelope filled with money out of his jacket pocket, and forced it into Hero's hand. Hero pushed it away, his face bright red.

Drew clasped Hero's arm and spoke to him intently as he pressed the envelope into Hero's hand. Amanda watched as Hero searched Drew's face. Drew nodded and smiled, and Hero squared his shoulders as if the weight that had burdened them had been lifted. Then he took Drew's hand and clasped it firmly.

Amanda moved closer, and Drew finally spotted her. "Amanda!" he called, waving her over.

Hero's eyes took on a wary, hunted look as Amanda stepped up beside Drew.

"Amanda, I was just telling Hero that you were the one who figured out that Tyler had messed with the computer." Turning back to Hero, Drew said, "You know, nobody really ever believed you took the money, Hero, although it did look awfully suspicious after you dropped that packet of money at the station."

"I never thought it was you, Hero,"

Amanda said, feeling shy in the face of Hero's indifference.

"Thank you," Hero said formally.

"As soon as this show's over, you can go claim that rattletrap motorcycle of yours out of the pawnshop," Drew said.

Hero's eyes opened wide. "How did you know I sold my motorcycle?" he asked.

"I told you already, guy, Amanda figured the whole thing out."

Hero sneaked an appreciative glance at Amanda, then quickly turned his eyes back to Drew.

"Now, let's get back to the business of selling tickets to these patient people," Drew said, indicating the growing line of restless ticket buyers behind him. "And later on, I have a surprise for all of you," he added happily, eyes sparkling.

Amanda and Hero looked at Drew quizzically, but he waved them off and joined the throngs that were headed inside toward the bandstand.

"Hero, I . . ." Amanda started to apologize.

"Here's your change, dude. Enjoy the show," Hero said loudly to the person he'd just served.

Putting her hand lightly on Hero's arm, Amanda tried again, more firmly this time. "Hero, we need to talk."

At the touch of her warm hand on his muscled arm, Hero's resolve weakened. He missed her, and he still loved her, underneath all the anger and hurt.

"Some other time, Amanda. Not now," Hero said in a low voice, keeping his eyes focused on the money he was exchanging.

Seizing on this crack in his armor, Amanda asked, "Meet me at Bluff Cove after the concert?"

Hero hesitated a moment, remembering their failed plans of last week for an anniversary picnic. It seemed like another life.

"Please?" Amanda asked simply, looking soulfully into the depthless brown pools of his eyes.

Hero gave a slight nod, unable to say a word.

"I'll be waiting for you," Amanda said softly.

The concert started a little after 6:00. The park was totally packed. It looked like everyone in Cliffside and the surrounding towns had come to the concert.

An expectant quiet settled over the crowd as Jamar burst onto the bandstand, followed by the other members of JellyJam. Grabbing the microphone, Jamar introduced himself and his band, to wild cheering.

"Now we want to thank all of you for coming out today. JellyJam here is going to entertain you for a while, and then we've got Jamie West's band, Jezebels, and Nick Ganos and Grim Reaper." Jamar raised his arms above his head as the crowd screamed in delight. Then, with one swift gesture, Jamar motioned JellyJam into action. Their music reverberated into the air, filling the park with sound.

Keera, who had been busy helping out with the food services, paused to watch and listen to Jamar. She admired his poise and confidence on stage, speaking and performing in front of hundreds of people. Keera knew she could never do anything like that.

Her father had been right, after all: opposites do attract, Keera thought. Keera knew in her heart that she couldn't possibly love anyone more than she loved

Jamar at this moment, as she watched him close his eyes and disappear into a world of swirling notes and bits of melodies.

Amanda came up to join her then, smiling about as wide as Keera had ever seen her.

"Amanda! What are you so happy about?" Keera asked.

"Oh, it's a wonderful concert, a wonderful day, and I just know that we're going to get enough money to keep broadcasting," Amanda sang optimistically, as she swayed in time to Jamar's music.

Glancing down at her watch, Keera realized that they were supposed to be meeting Jezebels and Grim Reaper in exactly two minutes. "Come on, Amanda, we better hurry," she urged.

As they rushed through the crowd to the south gate, Amanda thought she caught a glimpse of Tyler. She couldn't believe that Tyler would actually show his face at this concert after what he had tried—and almost succeeded—in doing!

"Is that Tyler over there?" Amanda asked Keera.

"I don't know, Amanda. What difference does it make? Tyler's a total disgrace," Keera remarked, impatiently scanning the gate.

"There they are!" Keera said in an excited whisper, leaving Amanda behind as she moved to greet the country's hottest rock stars.

Amanda hung back, suddenly shy. Without warning, an icy hand gripped her elbow from behind.

Amanda whirled around and came face to face with—Tyler Scott! Only instead of his usual khakis and cotton shirts, Tyler was wearing a parks services uniform, with a canvas carry-all strapped around his shoulder.

"Tyler, what are you doing here?" Amanda asked suspiciously. Was this outfit part of another scheme of Tyler's to sabotage the concert?

"Thanks to you, I'm doing community service, starting today," Tyler replied bitingly.

"Thanks to me?" Amanda asked.

"That's right. Weren't you the one who figured out it was me who deleted the money from the ticket account and sent the letter cutting off funds to KSS?"

"So, I was right," Amanda said.

"When your precious Drew phoned my dad—at your suggestion—ol' Tyler Senior hit the roof. He told me he would do me a favor: instead of sending me to jail, I'd have to work off my sentence, doing community work," Tyler said, practically spitting out the words. "So this is my life as a park cleaner, until further notice," he added, bitterly spiking a piece of trash with a pointed pole.

Amanda would have laughed out loud and told him that it served him right. But the fury in Tyler's eyes stopped her cold.

Just then, Keera, with Nick Ganos, Jamie West, and their band members in tow, rushed over to Amanda and whirled her around.

"Amanda, what are you doing? Nick Ganos and Jamie West are here. We're supposed to be escorting them to the bandstand, remember?" Keera said, insistently pulling her along.

Some day—some day soon—Tyler promised himself as he watched Amanda walk off, chattering a mile a minute with her famous companions, Amanda Townsend would have to pay.

* * *

At exactly 8:00, Jamar introduced Jamie West's Jezebels. They strode confidently to center stage, and the crowd went wild, cheering and chanting "Nighttime Vigil," the group's latest hit song.

"We just want you all to know that we think your KSS-Off Concert is almost as cool as the KSS-TV show, and we love ya!" Jamie shouted into the microphone, raising the decibel level to ear-splitting dimensions. Then, with a crash of guitar strings, Jezebels began their first set.

Keera was busy filming Jezebels' performance, when Jamar came up from behind, slipped his arms around her waist, and held her close. For a moment, Keera leaned into him, loving the feel of his strong arms wrapped around her.

"You were great," Keera said sincerely, turning her face and holding her mouth up to be kissed.

"Thank you," Jamar answered, basking in Keera's smile. "Girlfriend, I definitely have to get myself something to eat before the next set, or I won't make it through," Jamar said, eyeing the food stands.

"Go ahead, I'm busy here," Keera told him, turning back to the camera and checking the sound meter on the microphones.

"Make sure you're not the one filming when the finale time rolls around," Jamar reminded her gently.

Keera's eyes sparkled with excitement. "Amanda said she would take care of it."

Jamar brushed her mouth with his lips, savored the taste of her for a few minutes, and then headed straight for the food stands.

As Jamar wolfed down a hot dog, Hero came over and put his hand on Jamar's shoulder.

"Hey, dude, how are you doing?" Jamar said, genuinely glad to see Hero, but not sure whether or not Hero was happy to see him.

"I'm doing okay," Hero said. "Drew relieved me at the box office, so I thought I'd check out the food situation."

"Well, there's plenty of it," Jamar said. Then he paused for a moment. "You know, man, I'm sorry about . . . " Jamar began uncomfortably. "Well, what I mean to say is, are we still friends?"

"Yeah, definitely. Forget about it, Jam," Hero said, equally uncomfortable. To cover his embarrassment, Hero changed the subject, focusing on Jamie West.

"Pretty woman," Hero commented.

"Not as pretty as your woman," Jamar said, eyeing Jamie critically.

Hero's face darkened, his jaw knotting.

"How are things with you and Amanda?" Jamar asked casually.

Hero didn't respond.

"You know, that girl spent a whole lot of hours combing this town for you and pinning down Samantha and Tyler for what they did," Jamar told him. "I know this is none of my business— "

"You're right, dude, it isn't," Hero interrupted him.

Jamar pushed on relentlessly. "Whatever's going down between you and Amanda, you ought to know that there's no doubt that this chick is in love with you—totally and completely. She's the one who brought Tyler and Samantha to justice," Jamar said before Hero could stop him.

"Yeah, that's what I heard," Hero said.

Jamar shook his head, wondering if he'd even gotten through. "Well, I've got to split—my set's up. Later, man!"

* * *

It was 9:00, time for Nick Ganos and Grim Reaper to perform—and the crowd was ready for them. As Jamar introduced the band, the crowd screamed, and some girls by the bandstand fainted. Then the loud, haunting sounds of Grim Reaper filled the night, transfixing the audience for an hour and forty-five minutes of nonstop showmanship.

Every time it looked like they were going to stop playing, the crowd flicked their lighters, lit their matches, and shouted so loudly that Grim Reaper played another song, and another, trapped like flies in the web of their spellbound audience.

Amanda had been hoping to spend some time with Hero during the concert. But he'd made such a studious attempt to avoid her that she'd given up and busied herself by helping Keera film the show. She taped the concert and fed the canned material on the air between music breaks. She even interviewed some of the concertgoers to get on-the-spot reactions to the fund-raising efforts that were being made there tonight.

With only fifteen minutes of air time left, Amanda made one last plea to the television audience to call in their donations or contributions to keep KSS alive. Then she turned the camera toward the stage to record the finale—JellyJam and Grim Reaper playing one last song together.

Grabbing the microphone, Nick Ganos told the crowd, "This next and last song is by a very good friend of mine—someone I only just met, but whom I respect very much. You all know who I mean— Jammin' Jamar!"

The crowd began to whistle and stamp, chanting "Jam-min', Jam-min'" until Jamar stepped up to the microphone. His voice shaking with emotion, he said, "This song is for the person who means everything to me. Keera, I hope you're listening."

Keera, who had just walked over to where Amanda was filming, froze in her tracks, convinced that everyone in the park was looking directly at her. As the strains of "Keera's Song" played across the park, Amanda seized the opportunity to interview Keera.

"So, Keera Johnson, how would you

rate your experience with Student KSS?" Amanda asked in her professional reporter's voice.

Keera was overwhelmed by how much she loved Jamar, and her job at KSS, and Amanda and Hero as well. In that split second, she realized that, despite her mother's insistence, this all mattered more to her than studying, SATs, and college all rolled together. KSS-TV was where Keera wanted to be, and Jamar was definitely whom she wanted to be with!

Looking straight into the camera, Keera announced, "I can honestly say that this summer job at KSS has been the best time of my life. And Ma, if you're listening, this is for the record—I don't intend to give it up—not the job, not Jamar, not any of it!"

As the last strains of "Keera's Song" played out against the dark and the applause began to swell, Amanda stepped in front of the camera for one last time. "This is Amanda Townsend at the first ever KSS-Off Concert, signing off, hoping that Student KSS will be back on the air next week, as usual! Thank you all for your support."

* * *

An hour later, as the last remnants of the crowd trickled out of the park, and Nick Ganos and Jamie West had said their last good-byes to everyone, Drew called a post-concert meeting of the Student KSS staffers. They all stood on the stage, waiting to hear whether or not the concert had been as much of a financial success as it had been a good time, or if this was truly going to be their last meeting together.

Drew told them that all the receipts were in and he had the grand total in his hand. "After paying for city permits to use the park, renting the bandstand and seats . . . "

Amanda groaned as Drew took his time, listing every deduction against their receipts. Hero gave her a quick, sympathetic smile, and Amanda's heart lifted just a little with hope, at least for them.

"The grand total is $12,934—or a surplus of almost $3,000!" Drew said with a flourish.

At first, nobody said a word. They were all stunned. Then Jamar let out a whoop and grabbed Keera, whirling her around in a frenzy. Keera started laughing and crying, not knowing whether the tears were from happiness or just plain relief.

Amanda wanted to go over to Hero and give him a hug. But when she looked over to where he had just been standing, she realized he had vanished.

"And that's not all . . ." Drew said, breaking into Jamar's victory dance. "After speaking with Mr. Tyler Scott, Senior, he has agreed that Scott Enterprises will fund the entire Student KSS program for the whole school year!" Drew told them proudly. "So the jobs are yours during the year as well, if you want them."

"Do we ever!" Amanda said, flying into Drew's arms and hugging him.

Keera and Jamar looked happily at each other. They would have a whole year of working together at KSS, away from Keera's mother and out from under the influence of Rogue. *We just might have a chance after all,* Keera thought to herself as she floated into Jamar's arms. Jamar held her tight, to make sure that, this time, she would never get away.

"So, I'll see you all bright and early Monday morning," Drew reminded them as the three staffers started to walk out of the park. "Somebody tell Hero," he remarked.

I will, Amanda said to herself. That is, if I get the chance.

Amanda waited on the farthest point of Bluff Cove, hoping against hope that Hero would come. Just last Saturday, she and Hero had been planning their first-month anniversary picnic, she thought.

What a wreck her life was, Amanda said to herself. Her relationship with Hero was completely ruined, Samantha was a total liar, and she probably never was a real friend, and Tyler . . . Amanda didn't even have any words to describe how she felt about Tyler and what he had done.

Glancing at her watch, Amanda realized she'd been waiting at Bluff Cove for over an hour. It was nearly midnight, and she was chilled. "I might as well give up," Amanda said aloud. "He's definitely not coming." Then a terrible thought occurred to her. Could Tyler have anything to do with Hero not showing?

Worried that something might have happened to Hero, Amanda turned to go. Just then a voice from beyond the bluff called, "Hot dogs, sodas. Get your ice-cold hot dogs and your nice warm sodas here."

"Hero?" Amanda called in surprise.

A motorcycle engine roared as Hero tore over to Amanda's side, hot dogs and sodas packed into his helmet, which was dangling from his arm.

"Oh, Hero, it is you," Amanda cried, wrapping her arms around him tightly as though she would never let him go.

"Hey, Amanda," Hero said roughly, not wanting her to know how close he was to tears.

"What took you so long? I thought you weren't coming," Amanda whispered against his ear.

"I had to get my cycle out of that pawnshop before I could come here," Hero explained sheepishly. "I just couldn't let it stay in that place for one more day."

Amanda gently took his face in her hands and looked hard into his deep, dark eyes. "I, Amanda Townsend, do solemnly swear never to let anyone or anything come between us again," she vowed.

Taking Amanda's face in his hands, Hero returned Amanda's look and repeated, "I, Hero Montoya, do solemnly swear never to let anyone or anything ever come between us again . . . except for my motorcycle," he added with a grin, unable to resist teasing Amanda.

Amanda gave him a playful smack on the shoulder. Grabbing her arm, Hero brought her fingers to his lips and held her hand against his roughened cheek.

"I love you, Amanda, and nothing will ever change that," Hero told her gravely.

Amanda closed her eyes gratefully. That was all she had ever wanted to hear him say. Wordlessly, Amanda moved into Hero's arms.

They knelt down on the bluff, Hero's arms enclosing Amanda, keeping her warm. Together they gazed out over the ocean as the night clouds parted and the moon gleamed brightly upon the gently rolling waves.

Amanda tilted her head up as Hero lowered his. At long last, their lips met, gently at first, and then with a passion so great it took their breath away.

"Happy anniversary, Hero," Amanda said simply, looking lovingly into his eyes.

"Happy anniversary, Amanda," Hero replied.